I0654612

THE SEARCH FOR KELLY'S HEROES

INSPIRED BY TRUE EVENTS

The Search for
KELLY'S
HEROES

CW5 ROBERT C. WHEELER (Ret)

AMERICAN STRIPES

THE SEARCH FOR KELLY'S HEROES
Copyright © 2025 by Robert C. Wheeler

This is a work of fiction. While real individuals are depicted, their actions here are entirely the product of the author's imagination.

All rights reserved. No part of this book may be reproduced (except for inclusion in reviews), disseminated or utilized in any form or by any means, electronic or mechanical, including photocopying, recording, or in any information storage and retrieval system, or the Internet/World Wide Web without written permission from the author or publisher.

Published by American Stripes
4781 North Congress Avenue #125
Boynton Beach, Florida 33426

FIRST EDITION

ISBN: 978-0-9857183-2-9

Book Cover and Interior Design
by VMC Art & Design LLC

Printed in the United States of America

This book is dedicated to all members of the Infantry, past or present, in all the armies of the world. Further, a tribute to everyone involved in the making of the movie, *Kelly's Heroes*: the entire cast, producers, directors, crew, musical contributors, and, of course, the author. It is one of my all-time favorites.

A huge thank you to everyone who helped make this book happen. I am especially grateful to Amy, my wife, Victoria at VMC Art & Design, and my friends Dr. Jeffrey Tunstall and Doc Hobson.

PROLOGUE

I'VE ALWAYS ASPIRED TO BE a detective and I guess you could say I have achieved that goal, albeit I am still a semi-talented amateur. No, to answer your first question, I'm not a Sherlock Holmes, Phillip Marlow, or Jim Rockford, nor am I modeled after them. I'm a retired Army Helicopter Pilot who finds it impossible to ignore a mystery. In the words of Popeye, "I yam what I yam and that's all that I yam."

The beginning of my story takes place in a movie theater in the Bazaar Shopping Center, West Palm Beach, Florida in March of 1970. My late wife and I watched the movie, *Kelly's Heroes*. I was shocked at the end of the movie when they got away with it. They rode off into the sunset **with the** *gold.* You see, I was raised in the era when the Hays code, instituted by the movie industry itself, ruled Hollywood pictures. The code was designed to keep the government from censoring the movies, but was more severe than any government censorship. One of the mainstays of the code was, "All criminal action had to be punished, and neither the crime nor the criminal(s) could elicit sympathy." The movies I had seen, up to that time, showed that the perpetrators of crime were not able to enjoy the fruits of their labors (even if they got away with the initial crime).

It *almost* showed the moviegoer the *real* world and some of the people in it: *Kelly's Heroes* proved to be a landmark event for me! I flew helicopters in Vietnam in 1967-68 and this movie showed that the ordinary soldier could actually win. That was something that wasn't apparent up to 1970. It made me feel good and that was all there was to it. So therefore, *Kelly's Heroes* has always ranked in the top five of my favorite movies.

Fast forward a few decades and I was visiting my nephew, Rod, at the White House Hotel on the Mississippi Gulf coast. I liked it because it is on Highway 90 facing the beach and provided a dynamite view of the Gulf of Mexico. It was May 2017 and Rod's stepfather had died in March. Rod and I hadn't seen each other since the 80's when he had been a teenager. We sat out by the pool and he talked about his stepfather. I hadn't known his stepdad very well, but Rod obviously thought the world of him.

His stepdad had held *Kelly's Heroes* right up there with

God, Mother and Apple Pie. It bordered on hero worship and he never would discuss his feelings about the movie with Rod, or anyone else for that matter. On one occasion when Rod had asked him why he felt that way about the movie, he had simply replied, "Impossible to explain, you had to have been there."

That one line had always stuck with Rod, so he presented me with a proposition. He would cover all my expenses if I would find out what, if any, connection his stepfather had with *Kelly's Heroes*.

The prospect intrigued me. I had been retired for 12 years. A good friend and I had written a book about the mysterious Amelia Earhart; I was always looking for a new mystery. This seemed to fill the bill. Rod told me that his stepfather had left him extremely well fixed and money was no object. Rod's parting words to me were, "Enjoy yourself, but find out what my stepfather had to do with *Kelly's Heroes*."

I promised Rod I would do my best and I'd be in touch.

I had no idea at the time, where I would go and who I would meet in my search for *Kelly's Heroes*!

PART I

CHAPTER 1

THERE IT IS! I THOUGHT to myself. It doesn't look anything like it did the last time I was here, 50 years ago to the day. Memories are flooding back. The house used to be called "The Carousel" and it belonged to the nicest lady I had known, Gayle Sheppard. The guys' faces, as they were then, came rushing back. JJ, Little Stevie, Robert Bobby, George, Mike, Peck, and Frank appeared as they did in 1967. That was before we all went on to do our time in Vietnam as newly minted helicopter pilots, courtesy of the Army Aviation Training Center at Ft. Rucker,

Alabama, 100 miles north. The outside of this Roaring Twenties style beach house had been updated with siding and a new blue metal roof. All the trim was either aluminum or freshly painted. The inside, however, was almost exactly the same as it had been back in the day: knotty pine walls, high ceiling in the living room that went all the way to the roof, maritime nets and ships' lanterns adorned the walls. The main entryway was through the kitchen and the back door opened onto a deck the width of the house and reached onto the white sand beach (or what was left of the beautiful wide white sand beach of '67). The four bedrooms (two downstairs and two upstairs) each had two full-sized beds. The three bathrooms had been slightly updated, but nothing major.

More memories jumped out at me as I opened the door to each room, so I poured myself a glass of wine and sat down on a chaise lounge on the spacious deck. This was where we all would sit and sun ourselves every Saturday afternoon, and invariably two or three pairs of girls would stop and ask, "Is there a party tonight at the Carousel?" And, with the leering smiles of 20 something, soon to be pilots, we would answer, "It's already started, come on in." And they would, every Saturday afternoon, and on Sunday afternoon they would leave. The house had been rented by men just like us for several years. A tradition passed on from flight class to flight class. It was just for fun because we all knew that in just a few months we would be fighting America's latest war. We were very certain that some of us would come back, and some of us wouldn't, and we were right.

I got up the next morning and put the coffee on so it could brew while I got ready to face the day. Unloading the car last night wasn't too bad, a couple of bags with my clothes and other essentials were readily unpacked and put in the closet and in the bathroom. I chose the same room that I had 50 years ago. I slept like a baby despite the memories of times past swirling around in this place.

After my morning ritual and gripping a steaming cup of coffee, I ventured into the living room where I had unloaded the 5 boxes of papers that I had acquired two weeks ago. The boxes were from my nephew, Rod, whose stepfather had died. He had left him his house along with 50 years' accumulation of life in the same house. Rod had been overwhelmed by the mountain of papers, books and memorabilia that his stepfather had accumulated. My nephew had moved out of his stepfather's house about 40 years ago and only visited when his mother had died in 2015. Never in a million years had Rod expected his stepfather to leave him everything in his one page will. The document had been short and sweet, "Rodney gets it all", which took up a whole page with signatures once it was put into legalese. Rod had gone through almost every one of the boxes over the next two months and had separated these five boxes from the others for me to deal with. The bank accounts, stock brokerage accounts and safety deposit boxes (that's right, plural) had been emptied.

The estate had been very involved and the money didn't come complete with a paper trail to reveal where it had come from. All in all, it was an estate worth well over 20 million dollars! This from a man who Rod had assumed owned only a restaurant and laundromat in Mena, Arkansas that was acquired after he came home from World War II. As luck would have it, he had actually owned 20 fast food restaurants in as many towns, and three car dealerships in Dallas, Ft. Worth and Waco, Texas. Also, there was stock in a bank in Switzerland and stock in some auto parts companies in Mexico. After a month and spending $20,000, Rod had gotten a report that showed all the money in the estate was accounted for, all the taxes paid and, seemingly, all was above board and legal. There was a catch! The source of the startup money for his first business was a bit cloudy. It was an above board loan from a venture capital firm in the Bahamas. That was straight forward, but the terms of the loan were somewhat obscured. Also, his stepdad's movements and residences after the war and until he filed his first income tax return in 1949 were still a mystery.

You might be under the impression that I am some kind of a detective or sleuth. No, I am not, but I am a pit bull when it comes to a mystery. I don't give up and I have developed a certain knack for uncovering the truth in many instances. Besides, Rod had agreed to pay all my expenses, to include this place for as long as it took to run down the answers. He could well afford to; he was 20 million dollars richer and getting richer every day. Why? Each of the businesses was still operating and showing handsome profits and the stock paid generous quarterly dividends. Of course, Rod knew that what I found out would go no further than the two of us.

I spent the next week sifting through the papers and trying to build a timeline of events. I'm sure that almost all of you out there have a period of time in your lives that would be very difficult to investigate, but this was obviously a deliberate cover-up of what Rod's stepfather, Bill, was up to. I worked from the time I got up in the morning, until three in the afternoon. Then I took my glass of wine out on the deck and enjoyed the afternoon and early evening before I went out to eat, a luxury I allowed myself on Rod's dime. After all, I wasn't getting paid for this effort so this was what one might consider remuneration.

Sadly, no young chickie dropped by and asked "Is there a party at the Carousel tonight?" That's what happens when 50 years have taken their toll on your body. Maybe…it is only Thursday afternoon… I'll have to wait until Saturday.

To answer your question, it's Sunday and no one asked if there was a party at the Carousel. Not really a disappointment knowing that I'm in my early 70's. Any young girl that wanted to party most likely had daddy issues. You probably aren't really interested in the youthful reminiscences of an old man. I had spent the last five days going through the five boxes that I had brought to this paradise. I must say, the old boy didn't give away much in the way of information. I had first looked for any record of where he was between 1945 and 1949 and came up with the sum total of zero. Next, I looked for a later reference to his time in the Army and found only one sheet of paper with some scribblings on it:

Kelly 35th Inf Div 340 MIA
Sep 44 Meurthe-et-Moselle

Not a whole lot to go on, but you gotta start someplace and this was as good a place as any.

CHAPTER 2

I HAD BEEN RESEARCHING THIS slim clue for over a week and had gotten a real education about the National Archives website. I'm glad I give 20 bucks a month to Wikipedia; they are invaluable. I dug in with both hands and came up with very little at first glance.

Meurthe-et-Moselle was the location of the 35th Infantry Division in September of 1944. They had landed at Omaha Beach between July 5th and 7th and entered combat on July 11th. They slugged it out with the Germans in the Bocage region of Normandy until the 18th of July. The 35th and 29th Infantry Divisions, at a cost of 5000 casualties, secured the high ground around St. Lo, setting the stage for Operation Cobra. Cobra was the breakout of Allied Forces from Normandy and the Bocage. I became involved in reading accounts of the individual battles of the 35th, 29th, 90th Infantry divisions and the newly arrived 4th Armored Division. Cobra was kicked off with a massive aerial bombardment by 600 allied fighters attacking a 300 yard strip of land near St. Lo. The second wave of 1800 B-17 and B-24 8th Airforce Bombers attacked an area 3.4 miles wide and 1.3 miles deep. If that wasn't enough, the third wave of 3000 B-25 and B-26 medium bombers bombed a small strip occupied by the Panzer-Lehr Division. This holocaust started at 9:38 a.m. and ended just before 11:00 a.m. when the infantry started to move. Inaccurate bombing by the 8th Air Force had killed 111 American soldiers and wounded 490.

Something at the back of my mind was nagging me. You know, like a tiny splinter in your hand. It's too small to pull out, but it works on you until you take a needle, break the skin and pick it out. Then Wikipedia addressed my concern. The 35th Division patch is a Santa Fe Cross in a quadrated circle on a blue background. It was the patch worn by the actors in the 1970 movie, *Kelly's Heroes*. This was my signal to find out all I could about the 35th Infantry Division.

At the same time I noticed that Oddball was wearing a 6th Armored Division Patch. Why was the 6th Armored Division chosen as Oddball's unit? This seems strange because the 6th Armored Division fought mostly in the western portion of Normandy, until it drove southwest towards the west coast of France. It remained there until participating in the Battle of Brest, which is just about as far northwest as you can go in France. It moved virtually unopposed to Saarbrucken, arriving on December 6th; then it became heavily involved at Bastogne during the Battle of the Bulge. The division proceeded to slice into Germany and ended up liberating the Buchenwald Concentration Camp and POW Compound in the north central portion of the Reich. It never fought in the Bocage country and as far as I could tell, never came near the 35th Infantry Division. A better choice would have been the 3rd Armored Division which was the spearhead for the 1st Army during the Normandy invasion; they fought through the entirety of the Bocage Country and supported the 35th and 90th Infantry for the breakout at St. Lo. But the 3rd Armored Division ended the war at Langen Hesse just south of Frankfurt in North Central Germany.

On the surface several questions were easily answered, but they required me to probe deeper. Who wrote the script for *Kelly's Heroes?* That was public knowledge. Troy Kennedy Martin, a British screenwriter born in Rothesay on the Isle of Bute on February 15, 1932 wrote the script. He also wrote *The Italian Job, Edge of Darkness,* and *Bravo Two Zero.* He died on September 15, 2009 in Ditchling, UK.

On December 4, 1968, Elliot Morgan, Head of Research for MGM wrote to the *Guinness Book of World Records* requesting information about an entry, "The greatest robbery on record was the German National Gold Reserves in Bavaria by a combine of U.S. Military personnel and German civilians in 1945."

The editor answered his letter on December 10th stating, "he had very little information and he essentially suspected that there had been a cover-up, which required that the story should be subject to a restricted classification…any film made will have to be historical romance rather than history." He said that would happen with the passage of time or change of classification.

The robbery and cover-up by higher ups in post war Germany that was later revealed in *Nazi Gold: The Story of the World's Greatest Robbery—And Its Aftermath* by Ian Sayer and Douglas Botting. Their research started in 1975 and is generally thought to be the basis of Kelly's Heroes. Several people have connected the *Kelly's Heroes* story to the disbursement of gold from the Reichsbank in Berlin to a number of locations around the Third Reich, mainly in the Kaiseroda Mine in Merkers, Germany. I noted that 8307 gold bars were found in that mine. This was supposedly the largest cache of gold from the Reichsbank. It was hard to imagine that *Kelly's Heroes* actually made off with 14,000 gold bars. According to IMDb, each bar would have weighed 436.48 troy ounces and at the 1944 price of gold at $34.00 per ounce, 14 thousand bars would have been worth 207 million dollars (not the 16 million referred to in the movie). However, 1,400 gold bars would have been worth $21,387,520.00, which was much closer to the 16 million referred to in the movie. But, did Mr.

Martin get his idea for the story from someone else or did he come up with it himself?

If the story came from the *Nazi Gold* theory, why wasn't the 90th Infantry Division chosen? It did, in fact, end up in Thuringia, which became part of the DDR (East Germany) where the sizable Nazi gold cache was found in the Kaiseroda Mine (near Merkers). Actually, the 35th Division ended the war in and around Hannover which is in North Central Germany. The best choice of a unit would have been the 45th Infantry Division which ended the war in Bavaria in and around Munich.

It is difficult to believe that a story about a group of grunts going AWOL from a combat zone to rob a bank can be traced to the book, Nazi Gold. It took Sayer and Botting until January 1985 to uncover and publish the story. Kelly's Heroes was released in 1970.

Shooting began on the movie in July 1969 and was wrapped up in December with about 20 minutes of the movie left on the cutting room floor by MGM. Clint Eastwood later said that the cuts would have developed the characters much more and have made the movie better. So, it becomes very difficult for me to make all those pieces fit together and that has always raised a red flag for me. It lends credence to the theory that someone fed Martin the story or at least the bare bones of it.

It didn't take long for me to start mathematical gymnastics. At 27.28 lbs per bar and 4 bars per box, it would take 350 boxes, each weighing 115 lbs per box (plus 5.88

lbs for the weight of the box). That is a whopping 40,250 pounds total or 20.125 tons. The typical truck used by the German Army was a Ford G917T with a payload weight of three tons. That means seven trucks would be needed to carry 1400 bars of gold. Each of the numbers would have to be multiplied by 100 if 14000 bars were involved. 14000 bars of gold would be worth a little less than three billion in 2017 dollars.

I marvel at the ease at which a movie's hero (or villain) can carry one million plus dollars in a briefcase. A briefcase full of 100 dollar bills weighs 22 pounds, plus five pounds for the case, equals 27 pounds. It is conceivable that a movie character could carry a million dollars easily, but any more is impossible in a briefcase. Five million dollars would require a duffel bag. Money isn't as light as we are led to believe. So, I think it is safe to say that probably 1400 gold bars were involved at a value of a little more than 21 million in 1944 dollars.

Was there a soldier in the 35th Infantry Division named Kelly? Yes, there were 39 soldiers in the 35th Division from the time they entered the European Theater of Operations to their exit December 7th 1945. So, one question from last week has morphed into 39 questions now. Unless I am extremely lucky, I will have to run down each and every one of them to prove that one, or none of them, is the Kelly from the movie. Of the 39 names, 16 spell their name Kelley and 23 spell it Kelly. I used the WAG method to decide which spelling to begin with. What's a WAG you ask? "Wild Ass Guess." SWAG is a "Scientific Wild Ass Guess." I save

SWAG's for really dicey problems; WAG is for mundane everyday problems. Kelly won the WAG coin toss.

My research has been pretty extensive, so far, but not deep enough. As with most investigations that I had done; initially with each fact uncovered, two or three new questions arise, and this didn't seem to be any different.

Rod wanted answers pertaining to his stepfather. The questions hung in the air every night after a day of research:

- What was Rod's stepfather's connection to the 35th Division?

- Did Rod's stepfather have anything to do with the writing of *Kelly's Heroes?*

- What was Rod's stepfather doing between 1945 and 1949? His service record isn't among his papers and no one seems to be sure what unit he was with or *if* he even served.

After two weeks, I've exhausted all leads to several important questions that have popped up. But, I have just gotten started.

CHAPTER 3

MONDAY AUGUST 7, 2017
The Carousel
Oleander Drive
Panama City Beach, FL

WELL HERE I AM AGAIN, older, somewhat wiser and living the last month of summer in a paradise. I have just finished my breakfast after I got back from my morning walk on the beach. It gets me going, somewhat difficult at my age. It took me a week to run down the 39 men named Kelly that were part of the 35th Infantry Division during WWII. Reluctantly, I finally arrived at the conclusion that none of the Kellys in the 35th Division were the Kelly of *Kelly's Heroes* fame. So back to the proverbial drawing board; in other words, consult the movie. One small thing had escaped me and it was in the promos. According to Wikipedia "…about a motley crew of American GI's who go AWOL in order to rob a French Bank, located behind German lines, of its stored Nazi gold bars."

I realized that the guy who fed the story to Troy Martin wouldn't have used real names, and if he did, the execs at MGM would have changed them to avoid any repercussions or legal problems after the film's release. It only took me a *whole* week to come up with *that* revelation. I had to start my research all over again.

Suddenly, while watching the sunset with a glass of wine, it hit me like the proverbial ton of bricks or a Mohammad Ali straight right punch that put Liston and Forman down. AWOL was the operative word in this scenario and how do you go AWOL in a combat zone…come on, I'm not gonna feed you the whole thing with a spoon. That's it! MIA, missing in action, the entire group would have been reported MIA and that was where I went next: look for the people reported MIA by the 35th Division.

It was kinda involved, this line of investigation. First I had to get a name from the 35th Division Archives of MIA's and then I had to look for a group of men who had gone missing at the same time during the August-October 1944 time frame. Not terribly difficult; sometimes ten, fifteen, twenty guys went missing on the same day in the same place. Then each name had to be checked in later MIA rosters to see if they had been removed from MIA to KIA (killed in action) or RTD (Returned to Duty) status. Then I checked the passenger lists for any of the men who had eventually gone home with the division. Finally, I checked the current MIA's with the Library of Congress to see if they were still listed as MIA. Now I have a list of 16 names that fit the bill. I have done preliminary verification of them and so far, the results were very encouraging.

The next 3 days, in a word, "sucked." I had the research protocol down pat and all I needed to do was come up with a list of MIA's by date from the 3rd Armored Division. The problem that raised its ugly head is there are no rosters of members of the 3rd Armored Division like there were for the 35th Infantry Division. So it looks like I have to plan a future trip to the National Archives in Washington, DC. I would have to spend the rest of my time in this paradise to gather as much information as possible on the list of names that I had.

This next phase was not very encouraging either. I did a preliminary search of the names I had and 8 out of the 14 that I found had one thing in common. They were deceased! I came up with a form letter and fired off a copy to each man's family members or anyone who could be familiar with his past.

Nick Wallach
My Address

Date

Addressee
Address

Re: Information for my upcoming book

Dear Mr. /Ms. Smith

I am a published author in the process of researching a book about the role of the 35th Infantry Division in Europe during World War II. While researching, I have found your Brother/Father/Grandfather/Husband's name on the roster of the 35th Division. I realize that he has passed on, but I am hopeful that he may have discussed his time in Europe with you or someone else that you may be familiar with. Any information you could give me would be greatly appreciated.

Thank you very much for your kind attention to this matter and I hope you will get back to me. My phone number is 000-000-000 and my email is N******@gmail.com. I also welcome letters to my address above.

Respectfully yours,

Nick Wallach

I sent out 62 of these letters by looking up people listed in each one of their obituaries. Then I set about trying to contact the four individuals that were still alive. In order to contact them I had to find out where they lived and hopefully could get a phone number. After 5 hours on True People Search.com I had the information I needed. Two of the individuals showed a nursing home as their residences. A quick phone call to each place told me I needed to send letters to their relatives because only families were allowed to visit. I suspected that relatives would eventually reveal they had some sort of dementia. I left voice messages at the phone numbers. I sent a letter to each of the remaining two candidates shown on the True People Search bios. Now came the part of any investigation that I hate...waiting for someone to get back to me.

I paced the floor for the next two days. I guess I was waiting for the point in the investigation when the hero, that would be me, would have an epiphany and all the assorted pieces would fall into place. This was also the perfect place in the story for the beautiful, blonde, busty love interest to appear and worm her way into my life. Sadly, neither of these things occurred. No epiphany but a really good idea emerged. After reviewing the people on my contact list, I started checking the obits again. Of the sixteen names, eight of them had something in common. They didn't go back to their home of record after the war was over. Most veterans go back to where they lived before their military service began, either to parents, wives or sweethearts. Why would these eight guys, who had been MIA for a period of time, not go home? So another question to be answered, but something told me that I needed to concentrate my investigation on these eight people, at least for now.

By the end of another week I had a large map of the US, delivered promptly by Amazon, and I placed sticky colored dots all over it. I had chosen a different color for each of the names and using a black, white or red pen I assigned each dot a number. The number 1 represented their home of record and the number 2 was where they went after the war. A piece of string between the two dots made it easy to keep track. I have always believed that women react to the written word and men to pictures. I don't think I'm wrong on this, at least it's true for me. Starting with JCB (no names please), his home of record was Newark, New Jersey, where he had a sister and mother that he had left behind. He moved to Omaha, Nebraska where, over the years he married, and had three kids-two daughters and a son. He owned a string of NAPA auto parts stores and five gas stations. His estate, divided equally between his kids because his wife of 56 years had predeceased him in 2015, was in excess of 22 million. He had married in 1959 and his kids were all grown and working in the family businesses. JCB showed no other relatives in or near Omaha, but several in and around Newark. It was like he had cut ties with his former life and started a new one in the latter months of 1945 when he came back from Europe.

The soldiers on my map came from all over the US and from all walks of life. There were fifteen Privates and one Sergeant and all replacements from different units in the 35th Infantry Division. Eight of them hadn't returned to their home of record, but the other eleven had. The only thread that connected them was the fact that they all had been MIA for an extended period of time. Later, I was to find out why.

This is a listing of eleven of the sixteen soldiers that I came up with. I have used initials because I don't enjoy the prospect of everybody from eleven families filing a lawsuit against me for defamation of character or using their names without permission.

+*JCB- 32***103-Private First Class -Alpha Company 137th Inf- MIA 12 Sep 44 Retd 1 Feb 45-HOR Newark, NJ- Born 4 Nov 21-Died Lincoln, NE Dec 12, 2002

*DHP-32***509-Private First Class-35thCavalry Recon Troop - MIA 12 Sep 44 Retd 1 Feb 45- HOR Northport, Long Island, NY- Born 11 Jan 24-Died Montauk, Long Island, NY May 14, 2007

*JPR-38***771-Private First Class-Anti-Tank Company 134th Inf-MIA 12 Sep 44 Retd 1 Feb 45 HOR Waldron, AR-Born 15 Nov 25-Living near Little Rock, AR Memory Care Facility.

+FRM-32***605-Private Delta Company, 137th Inf-MIA 12 Sep 44 Retd 15 Feb 45 HOR Denver, CO-Born 31 Dec 25 Living San Diego, CA

*JCK-38***895-Private First Class-Anti-Tank Company Special Troops 134th Inf- MIA 12 Sep 44 Retd 1 Feb 45 HOR Happy, TX- Born 2 Nov 22-Died Midland, TX Aug 17, 2004

*WJR-33***382-Private First Class-35th Cavalry Recon Troop-MIA 12 Sep 44 Retd 1 Feb 45 HOR Intercourse, PA-Born 15 June 24-Died Tinicum Township, Bucks County, PA Jun 18, 2009

+JAT-31***443-Private-Hotel Company, 137th Inf- MIA 12 Sep 44 Retd 17 Feb 45 HOR Cambridge, MA-Born 30 Jan 24-Died San Diego, CA Apr 23, 2005

+JJK-33***983-Private-Battery B 161st Field Artillery Battery 35th ID-MIA 12 Sep 44 Retd 20 Feb 45 HOR Pittsburgh, PA-Born 12 Dec 24-Memory Care near Groton CT

+SAG-33***888-Private-Fox Company 134th Inf-MIA 12 Sep 44 Retd 1 Feb 45 HOR Uniontown, PA- Born 2 June 25 Living Miami, FL

+PAM-33**8923-Private First Class-Mike Company 137th Inf-MIA 12 Sep 44 Retd 18 Feb 45 HOR Baltimore, MD- Born 20 Oct 15 Died Monterey, CA May 15, 2015

+RTM-R4***7715-Staff Sergeant-Kilo Company 134th Inf-MIA 12 Sep 44 Retd 14 Feb 45 HOR Pittsburgh, PA- Born 9 Nov 17 Disappeared NYC, NY

*-Deceased
+-Didn't return to HOR (Home of Record) in 1945

Now I had the remaining five to figure out, and so far, no luck. I still had the 3rd Armored Division to look through. There would be fifteen names, three tank crews to cull from the thousands that had served. This wasn't going to happen overnight!

CHAPTER 4

THREE DAYS AGO I WAS hit up the side of the head by an answer from one of my 62 letters. She telephoned me and simply asked, "Who are you and what do you want?"

"An author writing a book and if you will tell me your name I will fill you in on what I know."

"Betty Johnson."

"Betty R. Johnson?"

"Correct."

It didn't take a rocket scientist to figure that Ms. Johnson was not entirely warmed up to me or my reason for contacting her; so much so that the number showing in my cell phone was simply "restricted."

"I believe that your grandfather was WJR who served with the 35th Infantry Division during World War Two. Am I correct in that assumption?"

"You are, he was my grandfather on my father's side. He died back in 2009."

"Could we meet somewhere and talk about it? I'll buy you lunch."

That ladies and gents, is how I ended up at the Naked Olive in Kennett Square, Pennsylvania. She said "one thirtyish" as the time that she would arrive.

And when I asked, "How will I recognize you?"

She replied, "fiftyish with short dark hair." So I drove to Kennett Square and was led to a nice table for four next to a long table with two trees apparently growing out of it, Ficus trees, I think. (If you aren't sure what kind of tree it is, it's probably some type of Ficus). I told the hostess that I wanted a quiet booth, she was happy to oblige, much more so when I slipped her a nice picture of Alexander Hamilton. She became even more attentive when I told her I was expecting Ms. Johnson, "fiftyish with short black hair."

I wasn't expecting what I got with Ms. Johnson. Yes, she could have been fifty, but looked more like fortyish. Well-endowed, but not Dolly Parton busty and the picture of grace in tight blue jeans and a form fitting white blouse. Tasteful, but she wore sexy 3 inch heels which put her at a respectable five-eight. She was very pretty with dark brown hair, but the piercing blue eyes caught me off guard. I suspect her blue eyes were compliments of contacts, but who cares. The smile wasn't particularly warm, but it was friendly enough. I got to my feet and shook her hand when I introduced myself.

"I was sorry to learn that your grandfather had passed away, I would really have enjoyed talking to him."

"Thank you…we can start with you filling me in on what you know and we'll see if I can fill in the blanks."

"It looks like he returned from Europe on the Queen Mary, leaving South Hampton on September 5th and arriving in New York on September 10th, 1945. He was discharged on December 2nd, 1945 at Ft. Dix, New Jersey, and as far as I can tell he returned to Intercourse, Pennsylvania on December 4th, probably by train. I picked up some of his business dealings. It seems he worked at Berger Construction Company; they had a training program for returning vets. He left their employ in 1950 and started his own business after he got his General Contractors License in December of '49. He was in his own business until 1966 when his son, your father, went off to war in Vietnam. He and his son formed a corporation in 1968 after your dad got out of the Army. They began doing just about everything: buying and selling real estate, operating fast food restaurants all over Pennsylvania, West Virginia and Ohio. Also, owning, but not operating a road construction business in Missouri. Your grandfather had three children-two sons and a daughter: William, John and Jennifer, J&J were twins. Your grandfather passed away in 2009 at 85 years old. Your father died in 2011 at 65 from lung cancer. That's about it, I don't know who inherited the company or what kind of estate he left."

"You are entirely correct with what you have. My father did die of lung cancer, even though he never smoked, but my grandfather did. My mother gets a pension from the VA because they believe the cancer was caused by Agent Orange. My grandfather did work for Berger and probably would have continued, but he got a business loan from the bank; I believe it was for a lot of money. That enabled him to go into business for himself and later bring my father on board. He actually did that before my dad went to Vietnam. His estate was worth about 18 million when he died."

We made small talk until she came back with our drinks and we ordered lunch. She ordered the Mediterranean Wrap and I couldn't resist the Naked Burger. We got back to her grandfather while we waited for the food. Resuming, I asked, "What a great success story! Did your grandfather have any close friends from the Army that he kept in touch with?"

"Yeah, he went to a reunion about every 5 years. The last one was in 2000 and he said everyone was getting too old to make the trip."

"Do you know which organization sponsored the reunions?"

"It wasn't an organization per se, it was more like a group of friends that got together. They would go to a different city each time. I think each site was chosen because it was near the home of one of his friends."

"Where was the reunion in 2000, do you remember?"

"I'd have to think, that was 17 years ago and a lot has happened since then."

"It would help me a lot if you could remember as many as possible. It would help me locate his friends."

"It seems to me the one in 2000 was somewhere in California…what's the name of the town where Clint Eastwood lives?"

"Carmel by the Sea."

"That's it!"

"Where did they stay while they were there?"

"It was a hotel on the beach, really expensive…I don't remember the name."

A quick look at my phone and *Carmel Beach Hotel* popped up. I showed it to her and she said, "I think that's it but I can't be absolutely sure."

"Can you think of anything else that might help me?" I asked, finishing off my Naked Burger.

"Not really."

"Do you know the name of the bank where he got the loan that he used to start his own business?"

"Neither my husband nor I knew where he borrowed the money. He wasn't forthcoming with most of his business dealings. It wasn't a local bank, of that I'm sure, but I don't know which bank, or where it is, sorry."

"Did you find anything in his papers after he passed?"

"No, there wasn't much from the early days, in fact I don't think there was much before he and my father incorporated. I don't think even my mother or my grandmother knew."

"Ms. Johnson, it has been a truly delightful afternoon and you are, whether you know it or not, a wealth of information. I apologize if I have given you any difficult moments opening up the past like this."

"Not at all, Nick, it has been a welcome change from my usual work load. You asked who inherited the business. My mother and I. I handle the office, mostly, we use a management company. Granddad did everything he could to provide for us. He made sure we wanted for nothing. The businesses are very profitable, but they require a lot of attention, if you know what I mean?"

"I do, here is my card if you think of anything that might lead me to his friends. If you come up with the locations of some of his reunions please get in touch."

"I will, it has been very nice." She got up and shook my hand. *I think her grandfather would be very proud.* Under other circumstances I would have asked her out, but I didn't want to take the chance of screwing up the only real lead I had so far, even though her smile was decidedly warmer than when we first met.

That night in my hotel room I went over my notes trying to put together something from the few facts that I had gathered. Some of these guys came back and went on with their lives. Some of them went to other parts of the country and made new lives. I needed to talk to someone who was left behind and find out how they reacted to this slight. Were there any bad feelings between them? Did the soldier stop all contact with his family and friends that he had grown up with? Again, I was like a dung beetle, rolling a ball of dung, gathering questions while searching for answers. Something was wrong and I didn't know what it was. I had sent letters to a whole list of names and addresses; so far only one had responded. It was time to start knocking on doors.

CHAPTER 5

I HAD DECIDED TO START at Baltimore, since I was already fairly close and work my way north to Long Island, then to Connecticut and finally Cambridge, Massachusetts. I had addresses to check out so I will knock on some doors. This method is like standing on a street corner asking every woman that passes by if she wants to have sex with you. You are going to get slapped and yelled at a lot, but you are eventually gonna get laid!

I was on my third house. The first two had basically told me to piss up a rope. Maybe the third time will be the charm. A nice looking lady in her early to mid-sixties answered the door. She had short gray hair, nicely styled. She appeared to be a bit overweight. Dressed in sweatpants and a loose blouse, her clothing revealed nothing of what was underneath.

"Good afternoon, my name is Nick Wallach and I sent you a letter last month inquiring about your uncle, PAM."

"Of course, I remember the letter, but I thought it was a scam and didn't respond. Obviously it isn't if you went to all the trouble to knock on my door. What can I do for you? Please pardon me for not remembering what the letter was about, old age and memory, you know."

"Yes ma'am, I am writing a book about the 35th Infantry Division and I'm gathering stories about some of its soldiers. Could we possibly talk inside or maybe I could buy you lunch nearby?"

"Please forgive me, come in by all means. Please ignore the mess, I have not been well recently and have had little time to clean the house. May I offer you something to drink?"

"No thank you, Ms. Jenkins I'm fine." I took a quick look around and concluded that if this was messy, then I was living in a pigsty. The small apartment was neat as a pin.

"What do you want to know about PAM, such a waste? We don't know exactly what happened, but what we do know smells of a cover-up."

Whoa, what does she mean by that? "Excuse me, but what do you mean by that?"

"You must know about his history, otherwise you wouldn't be here."

"No ma'am I do not. I don't have access to his service records."

"Well my father did, he wrote a letter claiming to be his brother and got them from St. Louis."

"Claiming to be his brother?" My face gave away my surprise.

"He was a foster child. Our family was the last one that he had lived with before he turned 18, so we were the only family he knew. He left my father his GI Life Insurance.

"Is it possible for me to see his records?"

"I don't have them, but my father did. He has been trying to find out exactly what happened. It was a mess and no one seemed to be able to answer the questions Dad raised, not to his satisfaction anyway."

"What questions?"

"Was he really dead?"

This was a totally unexpected turn of events and I hoped that my shock didn't register on my face, but apparently it did.

"You didn't know?"

"No ma'am, I didn't. My research shows he went missing on September 12th and was returned to US control on February 18, 1945. I show that he returned on the *SS Cristobal*, arriving in Boston on August 31st and was most likely discharged a month or two later."

"I agreed until the part about his being returned to US control. We learned that he was declared Killed in Action on January 15, 1945 and buried in the American Cemetery d'Epinal between Arches and Le Champ-du-Pin, France. We have the paperwork, but Dad also picked up another report, purely by chance, that he returned on the *SS Cristobal*. He was discharged on December 15th, 1945 at Ft. Dix, New Jersey. So, we wonder which one is correct?"

I couldn't answer her honestly. I have information that he died July 15, 2015 in Monterey, California which would open another can of worms for her and her father. I had to think about this.

"Is it possible to talk with your father?"

"Not a good idea, he is 85 and not in good health. We, the family, believe he has a touch of dementia and he doesn't think about his "brother" every waking minute of every day like he used to. Better to let sleeping dogs lie. I will get the documents of my "uncle's" death, copy them and mail them to you. You will need back up documentation, I know, I used to have to deal with publishers and authors when I was working."

"Who did you work for, if I may ask?" I handed her my card with the address of my mail drop in Florida.

"A DC Attorney, big wig. They used to like to sue authors and publishers who went loose with the facts." She said as she read my card.

"Then I'd better watch my step."

"Yes, you better, not from our point of view, but other people may sense a deep pocket and that's what attorneys are drawn to."

"Thank you very much Ms. Jenkins for your information and the advice, both are greatly appreciated."

"A pleasure, Nick, I hope you find out more. Can I count on you to keep me informed?" She waved my card in the air.

"You sure can, have a good rest of your day." She smiled and shook my hand. I turned and walked to my car. I could sense her watching me and I waved at her as I pulled away from the curb.

I dragged out all my research that night to try to make sense of what I knew so far. I had to make sure that PAM was really KIA. If he was, that meant that someone came back to the States using his name and service record. If he wasn't KIA, which was more likely, he had deserted his foster family and played dead for some reason. Either way, there was a mystery that needed to be solved. It raised another red flag, something wasn't Kosher here. I got on my computer and typed in PAM's information on the American Battle Monuments website. I wasn't really ready for what popped up.

"Last Name, First Name, Middle Initial, Rank, Service Number, Branch, World War 2, d'Epinal Cemetery, Entered Service from Baltimore, MD, 137th Infantry Regiment, 35th Infantry Division." I clicked on his last name and it gave his date of death, the plot, row, grave number and cemetery where he was buried. It also listed his awards.

Now we have a new wrinkle, PAM was KIA on January 15, 1945, but somehow managed to sail on the *SS Cristobal* on August 23, 1945 and be discharged on December 15th at Ft. Dix, New Jersey. As Sherlock Holmes said, "When you have eliminated the impossible, whatever remains, however improbable, must be the truth." This situation was a perfect example. Someone assumed PAM's identity and kept it until he died on July 15, 2015 in Monterey, California.

I mulled this whole scenario over in my mind for the rest of the evening. How easy would it have been to steal someone's identity in Europe during World War II? The answer was...very easy if you worked in the Personnel Section of the 35th Division or any other Army unit in Europe between June 1944 to June 1945. I called a friend of mine from my military days who had worked in personnel. He assured me that if you were in the right position you could invent a person, show him as ready for duty and collect his pay (which direct deposit had made much easier). Until the military became computerized in the late nineties, it was a cinch. The problem was that the Personnel Section of the 35th Division had to manifest about 2300 troops on that ship and there wasn't the time or the manpower to make cross checks on everyone for accuracy. The 137th was on the *SS Cristobal*, whereas the *Queen Mary* held over 16,000, over half of which were 35th Division troops. The more I thought about that, the more I realized just how easy it would have been for the right person in the right position. I had to interview someone who was still alive and, as a good friend of mine used to say, "we're burning daylight."

CHAPTER 6

THE REST OF MY TRIP had been a bust; no one would talk to me. I had decided not to look in on JJK in Groton, Connecticut because I couldn't get permission from his family to visit. Pulling a Jim Rockford, glibly talking my way into his room or breaking and entering, just wasn't my cup of tea. Back in Panama City Beach I reluctantly packed my bag, threw it in the trunk of my 2000 SL 500, and got in. I took a long look at "The Carousel" and put the top down because what's the use of having a convertible in Florida, if you drive with the top up?

I spent the last week since returning to "The Carousel" nailing down a list of people who might fit the "still alive" category that I could talk to. I had also done quite a bit of research on identity theft and how far back it went. To my surprise, its earliest recorded incident was in 1548 with the theft of Martin Guerre's identity by Arnaud du Tilh. Arnaud didn't fare too well because he was found out, tried, convicted, and hanged in front of Guerre's house. I feel quite certain that victims of identity theft today would like to see the perpetrators of their thefts receive the same treatment.

ID theft today should be getting harder and harder. The public is informed and with computers and constant vigilance by watchdog agencies it should be close to impossible, right? Sorry guys, it's epidemic, so much so that people are afraid to open a file on their computers or even read an email from someone they don't know. Typically, people don't answer their phones unless the name of the caller appears on their screen or they know the number. We live in an age when we can call or email around the globe to anyone we wish, yet we are afraid to open messages, answer the phone, or send a check through the mail. All this is very sad, but very true.

Not something for me to worry about. I spent the next three days driving along the coast road, US Highway 98 to be exact, top down, enjoying the sights of the Florida panhandle, Mobile, Alabama, the Mississippi Gulf Coast, and New Orleans, my present destination. I needed to talk to PAM's daughter or one of her grown sons. They lived near each other in the Garden District according to True People Search.com.

I drove to the French Quarter and got a room at my favorite hotel, Place d'Armes which is next to the St. Louis Cathedral on Jackson Square-hard to get much closer to the heart of the Quarter. A very pretty, slim, 25ish girl with cocoa brown skin, flowing black hair and green eyes that you could easily get lost in, smilingly gave me a third floor room overlooking the courtyard with its pool and fountain. I suspected that she had an equally good looking boyfriend, husband or girlfriend, although something in her manner said no girlfriend. I thought that even 50 years ago I wouldn't have stood a chance, oh well; such is life in the big city, sometimes even the birds end up walking. The garage attendant smilingly took my keys and I watched as he drove it into an elevator and took it to God knows where. I didn't care, NOLA isn't a city that you drive in, either you walk or ride the streetcar, train, or even a trolley.

I left the hotel after unpacking and walked across Jackson Square. It was late afternoon and it brought back a childhood memory of my first time here with my mother and brothers. I still can hear the tortured trumpet wailing with, what I would later learn, was New Orleans Blues coming from one of the apartments overlooking the Square. It wasn't this crowded in 1959 and I was only 15 years old, but this is the memory that comes to me every time I think about this vibrant city. One of two cities in the world that I adore, the other being Salzburg, Austria, they have much the same exciting vibe.

I turned right on Decatur Street in front of the old Jax

Brewery. I still remember the foul smell from 1959, but it has since been converted into shops and restaurants. I dare say that probably not a single person shopping or eating there remembers the old Brewery and how it smelled and looked. I turned left on Toulouse Street and made my way to the Toulouse Street Trolley station. I presented my 1 day Senior Jazzy Pass to the conductor. I had bought 3 of them online for $.80 each, without a doubt the cheapest and best way to travel in this city. It lets you have unlimited rides on all city operated buses, streetcars, and ferries. That, ladies and gentlemen, is your travel tip for the day.

I took the trolley to Canal Street and caught the Canal Street Trolley to the St. Charles Street stop at Carondelet and sat back to enjoy the scenic ride through the old mon-eyed section of NOLA. I kept my eye out for the house near Loyola University just off of Jefferson Ave. It was a beautiful old place near the corner. I had sent a letter to the lady that lived there that I was pretty certain was PAM's daughter. I got off at the St. Joseph at St. Charles trolley stop and walked back the two blocks to Jefferson. Jefferson is a divided two lane road with trees planted in the center median strip. They are young now, but one day Jefferson Avenue will have big oak trees shading the road. Someone was thinking ahead, not too much of that nowadays.

I walked to the door and rang the bell. I heard a voice through the door 15 seconds later.

"Who's there?" She questioned with what I would call a whiskey voice, an older female probably.

"Nick Wallach to see Ms. Chambliss, I sent a letter several weeks ago."

"Wait a minute please."

Three minutes later the door opened and revealed a rather saucy looking 60 something woman, thin, but not skinny. She had medium length honey blond hair with short bangs, all nicely styled. She was dressed in a Southern Belle's dressing gown (circa Blanch Dubois). She was good looking enough to make me imagine what she looked like under the gown. I suppressed the thought that she was naked under the gown (it would save me an embarrassing moment if she looked down).

She didn't take her eyes off mine as she asked, "May I do something for you, Mr. Wallach?"

"Yes ma'am, if you have a few minutes, I would like to ask you some questions about your father."

"Are you aware he has passed away?"

"Yes ma'am, I'm sorry for your loss."

"Don't be, he lived to ninety-nine and five months, a long life in anybody's book. I am his daughter from his second marriage. Please come in, I hope you will excuse the mess, this is the maid's day off."

"I'm sure it'll be fine."

"May I offer you something to drink, I was just making myself some coffee."

"That would hit the spot."

"Do you mind Chicory?"

"I prefer it," I lied.

She left the room and returned with a humongous silver tray with two Mikasa cups and saucers, a silver carafe, sugar bowl, and creamer pitcher, all very old southern hospitality. She poured me a cup and motioned towards the sugar and cream. I held up my hand to decline. She took a sip of her coffee as she sat down on the couch and nodded to the chair next to it. I sat down.

"Do you mind talking about your father?"

"No, on the contrary I would enjoy it. I'm sorry I didn't answer your letter, but both my sons and brothers discouraged it. They said it was probably a scam."

"It isn't, I assure you. I'm writing a book and trying to gather some background on several individuals that I've chosen to represent the 35th Infantry Division in the book. I'm especially interested in their lives after the war, you know, what did they do, how did the war affect them later on?"

"I would venture to say Dad wasn't worse for the wear. He married my Mom about ten years after the war was over. They met in San Diego and stayed together until she died in 2004."

"You said it was his second marriage, do you know anything about his first wife?"

"Very little, it was a taboo subject around our house. I do remember he mentioned her once when he found out she died, that would have been in 2013 or 14, I believe, but don't hold me to it. Her name was Joyce, but I think she remarried."

"Do you know where she lived?"

"Here in New Orleans to the best of my knowledge, in fact Dad moved my Mom and me here in 1983."

"Do you know why he moved?"

"Sure, he had just retired and said that ever since he was a young man he had always wanted to live here. He said he had been stationed somewhere in the South during the war. He came here on leave once and fell in love with the place. I think his work in California was the only reason he stayed there, instead of moving here. I suspect, no proof mind you, that he left for California to make his fortune and she, Joyce, didn't want to leave. I think that's what happened, but I'm not sure. More coffee?"

"If you wouldn't mind, it is delicious." She poured me another cup and I took a long sip. *Actually, it was really good.*

"What did your dad do out West?"

"I think he would have said a little of this and a little of that. Car dealerships, three trucking companies…"

"Three?" I interrupted.

"Yes, one was oil transport, one was a long haul, I believe, and the third was an air freight delivery before Fed-Ex bought him out. He had some orange groves in the San Joaquin Valley near Fresno, I think. He also dabbled in the stock market. I understand from the lawyers, that he was highly successful in the market and had a knack for buying and selling. He left me very well off as I get a six figure allowance every year to live on and according to the lawyers, the estate gets bigger every year."

"Sounds like he knew what he was doing."

She just smiled that, "wouldn't you like to know smile." We chit-chatted for another five minutes before she went to her desk in the other room to look for the name of her father's first wife. She came back with her name on a sticky note.

"Joyce Roberts?"

"That's what I have in my notes. I don't have any contact information, but she lived in this area the last time we spoke."

"Did you meet her or talk on the phone?"

"We met for lunch at the Café Pontalba down in the Quarter near Jackson Square about five years ago. We didn't discuss anything of great import, just chatted a bit."

"I know the restaurant well. I would like to take you and your husband out to dinner while I'm in town if it's okay with you?"

"No husband or boyfriend and I would love to."

"Court of Two Sisters tomorrow at seven all right?"

"I see you know where to eat in the Quarter, I'll see you there."

"It has been a pleasure Ms. Chambliss, I'll see you then."

"It's Jeanne, please."

"Jeanne it is, thank you again."

Back at the hotel I consulted my True People website and found a listing for Joyce Roberts, but it indicated she died in 2014. The obituary from Ancestry said she had two sons. Finding their names and addresses was very simple, but only one of them lived in New Orleans, the younger one lived in Fredericksburg, Texas. The New Orleans one was a law-yer, who, from the residence and office addresses, was doing rather well. His name was Hugh Roberts and he was the head honcho in the Banking and Finance section of James McPeak LLC-in business well before the Civil War and still going strong. That sounded almost like an advertising slogan. I made an appointment to speak with Mr. Owens because Mr. Roberts was unavailable. I needed to get my foot in the door and hopefully speak with Roberts later. The appointment was for the day after tomorrow, but to tell you the truth, I didn't expect much cooperation. I took the trolley to the St. Charles at Poydras stop and walked to the New Orleans City Hall just to have a look around and familiarize myself with the lay of the land here in "lawyerville." It's just a hop, skip and a jump from the Storyville red light district; something to be said for the semblance of the occupations practiced in the both locations.

I got back to d'Armes in time to shower, change clothes and walk to the Court of Two Sisters. It was a quarter to seven so I went inside to make sure they still had my reser-vation. The pretty young hostess smiled and politely told me my table would be ready in about 10 minutes. I told her I was expecting a lady friend and I would be in the bar.

"Will she ask for you?" She said with a fetching smile.

"I hope so, unless she has gotten a better offer since yes-terday." We both laughed and I went to the bar.

I was only a couple of sips into a glass of Pinot Noir when she tapped me on the shoulder and whispered close to my right ear. "Hey sailor, looking for a good time?"

"Always looking, seldom finding," I said, smiling and turning towards Jeanne. What I saw was not the picture of Blanche Dubois in a silk dressing gown, but a radiant mid-fifties woman in a low cut, very revealing black cocktail dress. I had mentally remarked on how her hair contrasted her well-tanned face when I had first met her yesterday. Now I could easily see that she must be tanned from her lightly made up face to her well-endowed upper body. Her hips were slim, her legs long with the same deep tan as I imagined, but couldn't see, under the short but tasteful dress. I recovered with a deep breath and with genuine praise I managed to say, "In the words of Fernando Lamas, you rook marhvelous Jeanne, look at you!"

"You don't look so bad yourself, most authors don't travel with or have an Armani jacket."

"I don't, I stole it from the desk clerk at my hotel."

We both laughed, she ordered a glass of Chablis, and we talked for a few minutes until the fetching young hostess appeared to show us to our table next to the fountain in the courtyard.

"I guess you haven't really experienced life if you haven't eaten in the courtyard at the Court of Two Sisters."

"I agree, I come here often, are you up for the Caesar Salad?"

"I bow to your expertise, Jeanne; I am in the mood for fish if you're taking the lead isn't a wet blanket."

"Au Contraire, I like to take the lead."

She summoned the waiter and ordered a Caesar Salad

and fish for me. Also, she ordered Shrimp and Grits for herself, and a bottle of Cabernet that, I'm sure, was going to set Rod back a pretty penny.

"I love strong women who know what they want."

"Then we are going to get along famously, Nick. Did you find out anything about Joyce?"

"Yep, she passed away in May of 2014. Her oldest son is an attorney with James McPeak's banking and finance division. According to his blurb on the website, he is quite good or that department is anyway."

"I hope so, they are handling my finances and as I said before, doing a great job. Not many people can say that three people can take six figures each out of a retirement account every year and it's still growing larger."

"Very true, do you know Hugh Roberts?"

"Not really, I deal with John Critchfield, but I'm sure if he works for McPeak, he is good at what he does."

We were interrupted by the waiter who pulled his serving cart beside the table and with a smile on his face he began making the Caesar Salad dressing. He started with the lemon, and after removing the seeds with a fork, he mashed the garlic, anchovies, Dijon Mustard and warmed egg into a paste. He then poured olive oil and red wine vinegar into the wooden bowl while mixing with the fork. Then, he added salt and pepper, torn romaine lettuce, croutons and shaved Parmesan cheese, tossing until everything was fully covered with the dressing. He moved it onto two chilled salad plates and put them in front of us. With a flourish he held his two foot long pepper mill and asked if we wanted more pepper. Jeanne declined, but I have never seen too much pepper on anything so I watched him grind away until I was satisfied.

We ate the salad and I thought this was the highlight of the evening until the waiter brought the Blackened Gulf Fish with Creole Shrimp Fried Rice and Pineapple Beurre Blanc. With the first taste I happily discovered that Pineapple Beurre Blanc was a white wine butter cream sauce with bits of pineapple; rich and buttery, with a sweet yet tangy taste, which was perfect with the rest of the meal. Her choice, Shrimp and Grits looked just as inviting. She even allowed me a taste and it was also divine. I offered her a taste of mine, but she was very well acquainted with everything on the menu. We both passed on dessert, but I think if we had indulged it would have been the Bananas Foster. We still had half a bottle of wine left after dinner. I asked her if we could leave with the opened bottle and she replied, "This is New Orleans, we can do whatever we please as long as we don't kill anyone too important."

I had to laugh at that and we caught a horse drawn carriage and did a tour of the Quarter. She pointed out all the important sights, bars, clubs and restaurants. We were approaching Jackson Square when I asked, "Where did you park your car, I'm sure he will drop us off there."

"I planned to have breakfast at Brennan's tomorrow morning, so I Ubered in, have any ideas where I can spend the night?"

"Driver…Place d'Armes please." As I said before, I really

love a strong woman who knows what she wants and how to get it.

"You don't play games, do you?

"Not at my age, when you're in your teens, twenties and early thirties you can afford to. But after 35, if you don't know what you want and how to get it you might as well jump off a building."

"I agree, here we are." She said, standing up.

"After you, Jeanne."

The driver's generic smile widened to a broad grin when I gave him a 50 dollar tip.

CHAPTER 7

FRIDAY NOVEMBER 10, 2017
James McPeak Law Offices
New Orleans, LA

YESTERDAY MORNING WE HAD BREAKFAST at Brennen's. The Strawberries and Crème as an appetizer and the Eggs Benedict were to die for. Jeanne and I had taken the street car to her place and she had, without any fanfare, had her way with me. Returning to the Quarter we spent the rest of the day lounging by the pool at the d'Armes and later, a fine lunch at Antoine's. I won't bore you with what we had, but the Classic Fish Amandine with the addition of Lump Crap and a bowl of French Onion Soup made me a lifelong believer in Creole Cuisine.

She changed into a business suit at her place and we went to see Hugh Roberts together. It was a challenging experience. Everyone was "business friendly" to me, that means they were civil and had plastic smiles, but they weren't what I would call friendly. We met with Mr. Roberts because Jeanne *was* able to get an appointment with him. It was all Roberts could do to remain civil after we mentioned his stepfather. I was glad Jeanne was with me because if she and her multi-million dollar portfolio with the firm hadn't been there, I think he would have come across the desk at me. The only thing we accomplished at the meeting was to discover that Hugh Roberts hated Jeanne's father. He found it difficult to maintain control of his emotions when confronted with PAM's name. Lastly, that left the other brother who lived in Texas.

Jeanne decided that she couldn't, or wouldn't, accompany me to Fredericksburg, so I took off the next morning early. We had breakfast at d'Armes and I dropped her at Harrah's on my way out of town. We promised each other we would stay in touch and I'm sure we both meant it. We will see what the future holds on that front.

I wasn't in a hurry so I took the route less traveled through Morgan City along the Gulf Coast, sans casinos. It was only a six hour drive without traffic. I spent the night in a quaint little motel in Port Arthur. I got an early start the next morning and I struck out in a northwesterly direction through Beaumont, the northern environs of Houston, onto Austin, and finally, eight hours later I arrived in Fredericksburg. The drive took me through some of the Texas Hill Country; compared to the rest of the state, the Hill Country offers some different and pretty scenery. I got a room at the Sunday House Inn that looks like a Swiss or southern German chalet transported from the old country. According to the desk clerk it was their last room. It was a King Executive Mini Suite. I took the clerk's advice and ate at Jack's Chop House. I enjoyed a scrumptious ribeye and a glass of Castello D'Oro Chianti.

As I ate I couldn't help but be transported to Villa Cheli near Lucca in Tuscany. It was an old farmhouse situated in an olive grove. When I ordered a steak one night the waiter/owner's son left the table without asking the usual questions. What do you want to drink and how do you want your steak? When I asked him why he didn't ask, he simply said, "rare and Chianti, this is Toscana; we don't do it any other way." The advice on Jack's menu, "The chef recommends all steaks be served medium rare," brought me back to Tuscany momentarily.

My research on the Roberts boys showed that Samuel was the younger son. He lived on Emory Drive and worked as an Uber driver and part time tax consultant. He volunteered in Company K at the National Museum of the Pacific War's Living History Program. I got on my Uber App and requested transportation to the Grape Creek Vineyards. I selected the favorite drivers section on the App and tapped Samuel's name; I had entered his name last night in the Favorite Drivers Section.

He picked me up 20 minutes later and started driving out of town on US Hwy 290. Samuel was a typical mid-fifties guy with salt and pepper hair and a mustache. He was thin, well built, with an ever so slight paunch. Blue jeans, white shirt and the black Stetson hat on the seat beside him completed the picture.

"Is it just a coincidence that your name is Samuel Roberts and you live in Fredericksburg, Texas?"

"I don't understand what you're getting at, sir."

"Samuel B. Roberts, Taffy Three, Fleet Admiral Chester Nimitz."

"Ah ha, yes, now I understand. My middle initial is "J" though and yes, it is a coincidence."

"I must admit to you early on that I'm going to get you to turn around five minutes after we get to Grape Creek and then you can drive me back to Fredericksburg. I wanted to have a few minutes to talk to you."

"Reference what?"

"It's about your stepfather, PAM."

I noticed a slight change in his expression through his reflection in the rear view mirror, but not near what his older brother had exhibited.

"What about him, why do you ask?"

"I'm writing a book about the 35th Infantry Division and he is one of the people I have selected to include."

"Okay, he actually wasn't my stepfather because I came along later after he and my mother had divorced. He sent money to her until she died, then the money stopped. My brother has never forgiven him for stopping the money. I don't know why my brother is so angry."

"Do you know of any written records that your mother may have had?"

"Nope, sure don't. If there are any I'm sure that Uncle Jerry would know where they are or may even have them."

"Uncle Jerry?"

"He's not really my uncle, we just called him that. He used to visit Mom every once in a while. Brought us all presents and just wanted to know what was going on with us. He was a good friend to Mom and PAM, that's the only connection that I know about."

"Do you know his last name and where he lives?"

"Yeah, I do, but I'd have to check with him before I could let anyone know."

"I understand, could you do that for me, it's really important."

"What's it in reference to?"

"The war."

"Vietnam?"

"No, World War Two."

"Here we are at Grape Creek, what do you want to do?"

"Take me back to town if you would and many thanks for your cooperation."

"Don't mention it. You mentioned Nimitz, are you a fan?"

"Kinda, I was born on his 60th birthday, the day after they raised the flag on Iwo Jima. His wife visited all the mothers in the hospital at Alameda Naval Air Station, according to my mother."

"Wow, that's something to write home about."

"Not really, just chance, like you living here with a name like Samuel Roberts. I study a lot of World War Two history. I've always thought of the *Samuel B. Roberts* as the little ship that never gave up when the chips were down, just like the guy it was named after."

"Yeah, I know the story of Taffy Three. There's also the fact that not many people know what happened, and they surely don't know the name; but everybody knows "Bull" Hulsey, the guy that hung them out to dry along with the troops invading the Philippines. Personally, if I were Chester Nimitz, I would have beached him in a heartbeat for that."

"I agree with you. He went off chasing four Japanese carriers that had only 110 aircraft between them. If I'm not mistaken, the Japanese had lost most of their carrier aircraft at the 'Great Marianas Turkey Shoot' in June. Halsey's actions endangered the entire invasion fleet. If it hadn't been for the escort carriers and destroyer escorts of Taffy Three, the Japanese would have made a sweep of the ships that were supporting the invasion. The *Samuel B. Roberts* was referred to as "the destroyer escort that fought like a battleship.""

"Yeah, I've read about Lieutenant Commander Copeland. He told his crew as they steamed full speed against a task force of Japanese heavy cruisers and battleships to include the Yamato, "...*we are entering a fight against overwhelming odds from which survival could not be expected, during which time we would do what damage we can.*" His men fought like tigers until their ship succumbed to three 14 inch shells and three 8 inch shells. She began the fight at 0700 and she sank at 1000 hours."

"It was an incredible battle with six escort carriers, three destroyers, and four destroyer escorts. They faced four battleships, six heavy cruisers, two light cruisers, and 11 destroyers; the Japanese turned tail thinking that they faced a much larger and more powerful force."

I felt that we had connected on some level. He didn't seem to feel the same way that his brother did. Our conversation had made the trip seem very short. He pulled to a stop in front of the Sunday House Inn.

"It's been great talking to you-I will try to get Uncle Jerry's permission to give you his contact information. Are you staying here long?"

"As long as it takes for you to give me an answer one way or another."

"I volunteer at Company K at the War Museum and I'll be there this Saturday the 18th. You ought to drop by and take a looksee; I should have something by then."

"Sounds good, see you then Sam, can I call you Sam?"

"Everyone else does, you're more than welcome to."

"I'm Nick, nice to meet you." We shook hands.

"Likewise Nick, see you Saturday."

I nodded and watched him get in the car and drive away.

I went to the Pacific War Museum and watched Sam put on his show with the artillery pieces used in the War in the Pacific. There was a 60 mm mortar and the pea shooter, that's a 37 mm anti-tank gun relegated to the Pacific War because its shells bounced off German tanks in the North African Campaign. Also, the 75 mm Pack Howitzer which was supposed to break down into portable pieces that men could carry up hills, over rivers, etc. I think that is one of the reasons I flew helicopters, that thing looks heavy. The military's definition of "man portable" and my definition are worlds apart. Sam did a good job and I actually learned something. My experience had only been with the 60 mm mortar and that's because I saw a poor grunt carrying the base plate which also looked heavy.

Sam gave me Uncle Jerry's address and phone number. He had told him I would like to see him in the next couple of days. I thanked him profusely for all his help and struck out on Hwy 250 towards Dallas.

CHAPTER 8

SUNDAY NOVEMBER 19, 2017
The Highland Dallas Hotel
Dallas, TX

IT WAS A SUNDAY SO I had taken my time, enjoying fall with its foliage colors of gold, orange, and red on Hwy 250. I drove onto I-35E a little south of Dallas and simply followed the directions of the pleasant English lady who was "living the dream" from inside my Google Maps App. She was really great once you wrapped your head around "turn right onto the slip road…" What she really meant to say was "Turn right onto the onramp…" But you know the old saying, "England and the US are two countries separated by a common language."

I mean who would call a cookie a biscuit? The Brits, that's who, and some folks that hail from Boston. "I'm going to the wardrobe, get my trousers, and trainers, so we can go horse riding; I already have my pants on." Translation: I'm gonna go get my pants and tennis shoes out of the closet so we can go horseback riding. I already have my jockey shorts on.

I had barely gotten settled in my hotel room when Jerry called and wanted to arrange a meet. I told him I was anxious to talk to him, so the sooner the better. I drove to his house on Wicklow Drive, near White Rock Lake and thought to myself as I parked on the street, *nice house, he is doing pretty well.* I did some research later and found out he pays almost nine grand a year in property taxes, rivaling California, New Jersey or New York.

I rang the doorbell and within a minute a trim, tanned 60ish man opened the door and smilingly said, "Mr. Wallach, I presume?"

"Nick, please, and you must be Uncle Jerry, sorry but that's all Sam called you."

"Probably because he has never known me as anything else, please come in. Can I get you anything? I was just making coffee."

"If you are making it for yourself I would be happy to have a cup."

"Cream and sugar?" He called from the kitchen.

"Black's fine."

"Me too," came the reply. He brought me a mug and sat down. I explained to him what I was doing and what I was looking for in as few words as possible. He listened, wearing a non-committal look on his face for the five minutes it took me to explain. When I was finished he smiled and sipped his coffee.

"Quite a project you've taken on, I take it you don't do this for a living?"

"Hobby only, mostly curious and helping my nephew."

"Several observations, if I may?"

"Please." *Maybe this is where the "big kiss-off" comes in.*

"You want me to fill you in on the details of a very large crime, if the movie is to be believed. You also want me to name all the people involved, even though, hereinto they have managed to stay well below the radar. Am I correct?"

"Yes. I think, well I'm pretty sure that the statute of limitations is up on the theft. Secondly, I don't believe the people they stole from are still around. Lastly, it is a gray area about the ramifications from our IRS as to unreported income, that doesn't have any statute of limitations."

"It seems like you have given this quite a lot of thought and are assuming a lot about what went on and what has happened since 1944. Oh, by the way, I think you are being followed."

Now that came zinging from left field like a bullet from Carl "Yaz" Yastrezemski's right arm. My expression must have given my inner feeling of complete surprise away. "Beg your pardon. How do you know that?"

"Don't feel bad, the people that are following you are pretty good. I would venture to say they have a tracker on your car. They're around the corner, off Kilarney on Tranquilla Drive, but there is no way they can see you now, or for you to see them. They're driving a black SUV, looks like a Caddy, not registered in Texas."

"Well Sherlock, that is quite impressive. Please explain."

He opened his laptop that was on the coffee table and turned it so I could see the screen. There it was a black SUV parked on the street with two guys in it.

"Do you have cameras up and down all the blocks in the neighborhood and how do you know it isn't registered in Texas?"

"Only two cameras are needed to cover the two approaches to Wicklow Drive. Also, the SUV doesn't have any front license plate which means it isn't registered in Texas; have you seen it before?"

"No, but then again, I wasn't looking."

"You should always be aware of who is or isn't following you. Cemeteries are full of people who didn't pay attention to what was going on around them. I'm going to give you some very good information before you leave here, but I have to be satisfied that you will be careful from here on out. You are dealing with things that you don't understand; some things could get you killed or at least hurt pretty bad. This has been kept secret since 1944 and it must remain so for the next few years."

"I understand."

"You have to, many people depend on your discretion! The only reason we have decided to bring you on board is because you won't stop digging until you have unearthed the whole thing and then we will have no leverage on what you disclose. Also, Jeanne Chambliss vouched for you, otherwise this meeting would never have taken place."

He handed me a single sheet of paper titled "non-disclosure agreement." It basically said I couldn't disclose anything to anybody about this story without the permission of "The Board." It stated that if I violated the agreement, I would be open to a lawsuit amounting to everything I owned or hoped to own for the rest of my life. I thought to myself, I wasn't sure I needed to know that badly.

"How binding is this?"

"The 'Board's' attorney wrote it. It's about as ironclad as you can get. It was written by three kids of the original group who have a great deal of 'skin in the game'. Are you thinking of violating the agreement?"

"No, but what if one of your guys talks, then what?"

"They won't, believe me, it would ruin their lives as badly as your life will be ruined if *you* violate the trust."

I nodded and signed the agreement. He took my driver's license and entered the numbers and the rest of my information in his Notary Public Book, notarized it, and left the room. I sipped my coffee until he returned. He gave me a folder, and in the words of Elmer Fudd, "Uweeka Gold at wast!" It contained a copy of the signed non-disclosure agreement and the information that amounted to much more than I could ever have asked for. We chatted for another ten minutes. I finished my coffee and got up to leave.

"Thanks, Jerry, you will let me know when I can publish this stuff, won't you?"

"Bet on it, everything you need should be there and will take you to where they crossed into Switzerland. You will need to talk with someone else to find out what happened after that. As Paul Harvey used to say 'Page Two' or the 'Rest of the Story', I forget which."

"I think I remember, 'now you know…the rest of the story,' but I could be wrong."

"What do you plan to do about your tail, the police?"

"The police? Not a chance, I don't have two or three hours to convince them that I'm not imagining things. Nor do I have the time nor the inclination to fill out reams of paperwork while they drink coffee and eat donuts. I have found that going to the law is a waste of time or a good way to get in trouble. If there is a crime, their first reaction is to think you did it. I'll handle it and thanks for the heads up. I'm usually pretty careful, but I never expected that this would piss somebody off."

"You will know why after you read what I gave you and guard it with your life. You already know the players and your list is pretty complete, except for Oddball and his bunch. Good story, that one." Jerry was smiling at the thought.

I left and drove past the parked car heading to my hotel. Tonight I will be very busy reading and carefully scrutinizing my car with a fine tooth comb. Hopefully, I could find out who was tailing me and why. This whole thing was beginning to feel more serious than a casual investigation into the distant past. I didn't like Jerry's reference to, "You are dealing with things that you don't understand; some things could get you killed or at least hurt pretty bad." I've been through three wars and had all the excitement/danger I needed or ever wanted.

I sat in the lounge at the hotel enjoying a glass of really good California Cabernet Sauvignon reading what I had just gotten from Jerry. The first pages were a rundown of Kelly's time in the Army. I hope all of you out there know the feeling you experience when you get confirmation that your hypothesis is correct. I have that feeling now.

KELLY

20 Oct 1915 (Wednesday) - Born Weatherford, TX. Oldest Child of MKM and MDM (nee F)

5 July 1921 (Monday) - Both parents died in an automobile accident near Ft. Worth. Went into foster care, no living relatives.

30 May 33 (Tuesday) - Graduated Weatherford High School, Weatherford, Texas

27 Mar 42 (Friday) - Joined the Army from his home in Weatherford, Texas and reported to Camp Wolters, Texas about 16 miles from his home.

10 Apr 42 (Friday) - Left Camp Wolters at 1005, arrived Camp Barkeley at 1525. 129 Miles from Camp Wolters to Camp Barkeley, TX (11 miles SW of Abilene) on US 80. He was assigned to the 90th Infantry Division

6 Jun 42 (Saturday) - Applied for OCS at the urging of his platoon sergeant. Designated Acting Corporal.

3 Aug 42 (Monday) - Finished Basic Training and was promoted to Corporal.

9 Sep 42 (Wednesday) - Met Board of Officers headed by COL Edwin D. Patrick. Application for OCS was approved unanimously

20 Nov 42 (Friday) - Left by train for OCS at Ft. Benning, GA

1 Dec 42 (Tuesday) - Started OCS in class #203

**13-19 Dec 42 the 90th Division participated
in maneuvers at Camp Bowie, TX (south of
Brownwood, 85 miles SE of Abilene on US Hwy 84)**

**26 Jan – 2 Apr 43 - Division moved by truck to
participate in maneuvers at Leesville, LA against
the 77th ID**

**29 Mar 43 (Monday) - Finished OCS, Class 203
commissioned 2nd Lt.**

**28 Apr 43 (Wednesday) - Reported to
Headquarters 90th Infantry Division Camp
Barkley, Texas (11 miles SW of Abilene,
Texas) Assigned as a 3rd platoon leader in
Item Company 3rd Battalion 357th Infantry
Regiment.**

**11 Sep-10 Nov 43 90th Division trained at the
Desert Training Center. Stationed at Camp
Granite, Arizona 40 miles east of the Center-
engaging in maneuvers against the 93rd
Infantry Division**

**1 Jan 44 (Saturday) - Division arrived at Ft. Dix,
New Jersey**

22 Mar 44 (Wednesday) - Division moved to the New York Port of Embarkation and boarded the *HMS Dominion Monarch,* ocean liner converted to a troop ship.

23 Mar 44 (Thursday) - Departed New York for Europe.

4 Apr 44 (Tuesday) - Arrived Liverpool England and transported by rail to Kinlet Park, Great Britain (near Kidderminster)

4 Jun 44 (Sunday) - Transported by rail to Cardiff, Wales where 3rd Battalion boarded the *SS Bienville*

5 Jun 44 (Monday) - *SS Bienville* assembled with the other ships of the convoy in the Bristol Channel near Swansea

6 Jun 44 (Tuesday) - Convoy sailed for France

8 Jun 44 (Thursday) - Convoy arrived off shore at Utah Beach, which had been secured by the 4th Infantry Division. The Regiment landed at 12:45

17 Jul 44 (Monday) - Relieved for cause, demoted to Tech 5 and then to Private

20 Jul 44 (Thursday) - Reassigned to 35th Infantry Division as replacement

Note: The official record shows that he abandoned his position, on 6 July 1944, when Item Company was encircled by enemy forces during the battle of Beaucoudray. He made his way with several enlisted soldiers across the swamp to friendly lines to get ammunition to take back to Item Company. He was kept from going back with needed ammunition by the Battalion Commander of the friendly unit. He had led soldiers through the German Lines with the mission to return with ammunition for the beleaguered companies. This was the testimony of the soldiers who accompanied him. The Board of Officers who relieved him couldn't verify the circumstances as reported because the entire encircled unit had been killed or captured. The Battalion Commander who had refused permission for him to return had initiated the Board of Officers.

Note 2: The Battalion Commander who had initiated the action was relieved for cause along

with MG Landrum and 15 other field officers during the period 30 Jul–1 Aug 44. This was because of inefficiency during the assault on St. Germain-Sur-Seves when the Division's attack had been thrown back by less than 30 German Paratroopers. 250 90th Division soldiers had surrendered; the largest surrender of the Normandy Campaign. This action was, however, too late to alter the decision of the Board of Officers who defrocked and transferred Kelly.

This revelation was dynamite! It proved the existence of Kelly, who had been a fictional character until now. The second gold nugget was a manuscript titled *The Warriors*. Also, I now had a starting place to see if there was a connection between Kelly and PAM. Tonight I would read Jerry's manuscript, *The Warriors* and tomorrow I would be on the road again. As a bonus I retrieved four trackers from my car. One was a burst transmitter which was hidden in the trunk behind the battery. It was hooked to the battery for electricity. There was a solar powered unit in each tail light behind the clear backup light lens. I guessed the burst transmitter was timed to transmit information every hour in a three second burst. The other two were continuous and easy to find with my SleuthGear Defender Bug Detector. The fourth was easy. It was under the right rear quarter panel in the wheel well and it was battery powered, rather low tech. I learned a long time ago that if you find one bug or tracker, you need to keep looking. You can tell how professional a spy is by how many devices there are and the level of sophistication of the gadgets. These guys were really on top of things. I could tell that the burst transmitter was the one I wasn't supposed to find. I would have to keep an eye out from now on.

The next day I installed a dash cam and hard wired it into my car's fuse box. I would be able to see who was tampering with the car even when it wasn't running. Next, were two battery infrared cameras with SIM cards and radar motion sensors. I hid one in the motel room. It didn't require Wi-Fi because it recorded to a tiny sim card, unaffected if the burglar had a Wi-Fi Jammer. That set up made it difficult to detect because it wasn't sending out signals that could be picked up by a Bug Detector. The second one was a standby in case I needed it.

PART II

The Warriors Manuscript

By
D........ "Oddball" S.....
and
L............ "Hustler" T...........

THE WARRIORS

CHAPTER 1

Near Flavigny sur Moselle, France
1 mile northeast of D570
2125 hours 8 September 1944

Kelly jumped out of the driver's seat of the Jeep that was hidden in the bushes just off the *La Vieux Moulin* across the Moselle River from Flavigny, France. Fischer and Grace joined him near the road. A five truck German convoy, loaded with infantry, had just passed the intersection headed southwest towards the bridge over the Moselle River that Kelly and company had crossed two hours ago. They carefully peered down the road and watched as the trucks pulled into a large field about a mile east of their position.

"Do you guys hear anything more coming?" Kelly asked in a hushed whisper.

"No, Kelly, just those five truckloads of Germans unloading in the field, otherwise quiet as a mouse living in Grand Central Station." Grace's voice was muted.

"Nothing towards Nancy on either side of the canal." Fischer's voice was louder than the other two, but still a whisper.

Big Joe, their platoon leader, who had been with the division Recon Troop since it had been mobilized in December of 1940, had ordered them to find an intact bridge across the Moselle River and snatch a high ranking prisoner, as high as possible, and rejoin them at their hide northwest of Flavigny sur Moselle.

The last quarter moon had started to rise at 2100 and was beginning to wash the rolling farm country of Lorraine with a subtle pale light. A light which they all knew was not particularly advantageous to their mission. When several clouds moved in to partially block the light, the trio seized the moment and started to move in the darkness. Intermittent showers soaked them every hour, but they only lasted about 15 minutes.

Kelly was becoming concerned about Grace's demeanor because he had been very quiet lately, but when he did speak, it was with an "attitude", as New Yorkers would say. Fischer hadn't changed a bit; he was matter of fact and an excellent soldier. Also, Fischer spoke fluent German, a product of his Pennsylvania

Dutch upbringing. Kelly decided that he would speak to Big Joe when he got back about getting another man for the Engineer section of the platoon. Grace was all that was left of the three guys that had been in the section when they landed at Omaha Beach. The other two guys had bought it trying to disarm some mines along the way.

Maybe Grace has had too much...maybe.

"Kelly, we got one coming from Nancy, he just turned onto the road that parallels the canal on the east side and I think he's lost."

"Grace, you cover us from the side of the road, Fischer you get ready, I'll handle the Jeep. What kind of vehicle is it?" asked Kelly as he started the Jeep.

"Sounds like one of those German VW Jeeps," Fischer whispered as he flicked off the safety on his M-1. Grace did the same. Kelly clicked the safety off on his M-1 Carbine and set it on the floor on his right side. They all waited, tensed with the rush of adrenaline as the vehicle approached. There were two figures besides the driver, visible in the moonlight as it descended the hill and before it started up the small rise to their position. The blackout lights were barely visible.

When the VW was about 75 feet from Kelly's location he revved the engine and popped the clutch. The American Jeep leaped in front of the German vehicle. The driver was very quick and swerved to miss him- but it was too late! His left front fender hit the Jeep's right front fender in front of the tire. The lighter German vehicle went into a broad slide and slid into the ditch on the other side of the road. When the German Kuebelwagen came to a halt, the man in the backseat popped up and raised his machine pistol. Grace put two rounds into the center of his chest and he flew back out of the vehicle. He landed in the plowed field next to the ditch with a surprised look frozen on his face. The driver was unconscious, slumped over the steering wheel with a nasty gash on his face from his right cheek to his left temple. The front seat passenger had hit the windshield and was out like a light.

"Get their weapons, throw the driver in our Jeep, and Fischer, you get in the German Jeep with Grace. I'll follow you back the way we came."

Fischer and Grace pulled the German driver from his seat and threw him in the front seat of Kelly's Jeep. The left rear of the German Jeep had hit the embankment and the left rear wheels were in the ditch. Fischer started the VW and smiled when it sounded all right. He and Grace picked up the dead man and hoisted him into the back seat of the American Jeep. Then Fischer pulled off the main road onto a small farm road and checked the front seat passenger to make sure he was still unconscious. Grace finished making sure nothing was left behind then got in the back of Kelly's Jeep with the dead German. Kelly crossed his fingers as the Jeep engine turned over several times; he almost smiled when it came to life. Kelly fell in behind the German Jeep and both vehicles headed towards the tree line on the edge of a farmer's field a quarter of a mile away. The entire snatch had taken eight minutes.

Fischer stopped and backed into the trees at the edge of the farmer's field. Kelly pulled up beside him and stopped. The German Jeep driver, an SS private, was just coming to. He was moaning and looking puzzled through the haze created by his wound and the blood that had run into his eyes.

"Grace, tie the driver to the front seat of the VW. What have we got here?" questioned Kelly, turning his attention to the man in the passenger seat of the VW, who was still unconscious.

"Obersturmbannführer....Totenkopf SS from his uniform. Das Reich Division, I would say."

"Very good Fischer, are there any papers on him?"

"Should be something in here," he answered, indicating a leather satchel.

"Maybe we hit the jackpot, but Big Joe's gonna be pissed when he sees the fender on this Jeep." Kelly eyed the crumpled right front fender. He then busied himself tying the unconscious Colonel to the seat in the German Jeep.

Ten minutes later Fischer said, "sounds like tanks on this road about half a mile towards Nancy."

"We hear 'em Fischer, let's get outta here."

Both vehicles started back towards friendly lines. They drove in the waxing moonlight. Near the field where the trucks had unloaded, trouble raised its ugly head. The German Army, namely the 553rd Grenadier Division was taking up positions on the west side of the Moselle River and there was a checkpoint at the cross-roads. Fischer in the lead vehicle turned around when he noticed the flashlights up ahead at the checkpoint. The armored vehicles were getting closer in their rear. They pulled into the sparse treeline between the road and the huge pond beyond. Fischer got out of his vehicle when they reached the trees and walked back to Kelly.

"What now?" he questioned.

"Strip both of these guys. Fischer, switch clothes with the officer, put him in the front seat of your Jeep and tie him up. Grace, you help him, and then put the top up on my Jeep after you help Fischer so the road guards can't get a good look at either one of us. Grace, put on the dead soldier's uniform and take the body back in the woods and dump it."

Kelly continued, "I'm going to change clothes with the driver, tie him up and put him in the passenger seat of my Jeep. Fischer, you tell the German driver that I'll blow his head off if he makes a sound. Let's get to it guys, it's not long till daybreak."

"What about the satchel handcuffed to the Colonel's wrist?"

"Wake him up, ask him for the key or cut his goddamn hand off if you have to; we don't have time for this shit."

Fisher shook the Colonel awake and asked, "Wo ist der Schlüssel?"

With a groggy look on his face the Colonel fished the key out of his pocket and handed it to him.

"Damn, that was easier than I thought."

"Get to it Fischer!" Kelly's voice was calm but firm.

Ten minutes elapsed until a column of three Panzers passed them headed towards the checkpoint. They fell behind the column and followed them to the check point a quarter of a mile ahead.

At this point, Fisher, dressed in the Colonel's SS uniform, was driving the VW Jeep. The SS Colonel was tied up next to Fisher in an American uniform. Grace was sitting in the back, dressed in the dead SS soldier's uniform.

Grace held the dead German's MP40 on the SS Colonel. When the tank column started to move, Fischer grabbed the German Colonel by the throat and in a low voice said, "Wenn du überhaupt etwas sagst, werde ich dich töten... Verstehen."

"Yes, Private Fischer, you will kill me if I say anything. Your German is very good."

"Thanks, a present from my mother and father," was his reply as he eased the Luger from its holster and held it in his right hand. He purposely exaggerated pushing the safety on the left side of the receiver forward and up, covering up the word *gesichert*. The Colonel nodded his understanding. He knew that being dressed in an American Private's uniform meant that Fischer could shoot him and not a word would be said.

The same thing was happening in the American Jeep, except Kelly didn't speak German. He simply held up his .45 and put his finger to his lips. Kelly was dressed in the SS driver's uniform and the German driver was in Kelly's American uniform.

Five minutes later they pulled up to the German Grenadier guarding the road.

"Wo gehen Sie?...Herr Obersturmbannführer!" Questioned the MP, snapping to attention as he noticed the Colonel's rank.

"Wir gehen zum Hauptquartier in der Nähe Creve Champs."

Fischer had made sure to tell him that they were headed to the Headquarters near Creve Champs, so the MP did not have to ask why they didn't use the road east of the river.

"Ist das nicht ein amerikanischer Jeep?" inquired the MP pointing to Kelly's Jeep.

"Ja, richtig, wir haben zwei Amerikaner gefangen genommen."

"Weitergehen, mein Herr."

Fischer nodded and proceeded slowly. The MP stared at Grace as Fisher drove on. He didn't see the holes in Grace's German uniform because he had brought the MP 40 up to his chest in order to hide the holes and blood stains. Also, the dim light helped with the ruse. The MP motioned Kelly through.

Fisher pulled off the narrow road out of sight of the

MP at the checkpoint and Kelly drove up beside him. In a horse whisper Kelly asked, "So far, so good, Fischer, what did you say to the guard?"

"I told him we had taken two American prisoners."

"Good, just a few more minutes and we're clear."

Fischer said the same things to the three young guards at the bridge across the Moselle and they drove into the village of Flavigny, bluffing his way through two more check points. Fischer turned right on the first farm road after passing the destroyed bridge in Flavigny proper and disappeared into the thick forest along the river.

Kelly stopped at a deserted barn near a field at the edge of the forest about 1000 feet before the village of Mereville. Kelly pulled the Jeep into the barn as Fischer parked the VW outside by the road making sure he did not block the driveway to the barn. Kelly took his rifle from between the seats and pulled the German Colonel out of the vehicle and walked him inside.

Inside the barn Grace, Kelly and Fischer changed back into their own uniforms. Kelly took two American uniforms from a pile in the corner of the barn and gave one to the Colonel and the other to the German driver.

Kelly was really glad to get rid of the driver's uniform because he had unfortunately wet his pants, probably when he was knocked out during the crash.

"Fischer, come here, I need to question the Colonel."

"No need Kelly, his English is better than mine."

"How convenient, Colonel, let's get down to brass tacks. What are you doing in this part of the country? The Das Reich Division isn't around here, or is it?"

"I won't answer any of your questions; according to the Geneva Convention I'm only required to give you my name and number."

"That's true so let's see what's in your briefcase."

A barely discernible shadow crossed the Colonel's face, but Kelly caught it. He pulled a black metal bar from the bag and set it on the ground. Then grabbed the papers from inside and handed them to Fischer.

"Give me an idea of what's there."

Fischer immediately began to read the tissue like papers.

"Colonel, it seems strange that you would have a metal bar in a satchel. Mind enlightening me on its purpose?"

"Disposal, if I had to get rid of it quickly I would drop it into the water and it would sink before my captors discovered it."

"I see, so you were going to uncuff this from your wrist, find some water at least three feet deep and throw it in before your captures noticed." Kelly's smirk was one of disbelief.

"Precisely, Private Kelly."

"Did you come up with anything, Fischer?"

"It's Orders and shipping manifests for 350 boxes of, what they call, priority cargo from some guy named

Max Heiliger to Switzerland. The paperwork is for a border crossing point at Delle."

"Does it say how big the boxes are?"

"Yeah, 18 by 18.5 by 10 centimeters."

"How big is that to an American?"

"My family was American, but we learned the metric system. It's approximately seven by seven and a half by 4 inches."

Kelly picked up the black bar and stared at it for a minute. "Correct me if I'm wrong, but that is about the size of 4 of these. How much does each box weigh?"

"Let's see.....52 kilograms... is about 115 pounds minus 5 pounds for the box, about 27 pounds per bar, give or take"

Kelly handed Fischer the bar and asked, "does that seem like about 27 pounds to you?"

"Pretty much," Fischer answered in his usual gruff, unemotional manner.

"Four per box and 350 boxes is..."

"Fourteen hundred bars." No one in the unit could beat Fischer when it came to math.

"Let's see what this really is." Kelly took out his pocket knife as he spoke and scraped away the black paint. He lit a match to see what was underneath and whistled softly as he handed the bar to Fischer, who showed it to Grace.

"It sure as hell looks like gold to me." Fischer was the only one capable of speech.

"I don't know what gold is worth, but I bet it's more

than a buck ninety eight an ounce." Kelly said and turned towards the Colonel who hadn't changed expressions.

"It won't do you any good Private Kelly, you don't know where to look."

"Not yet, but soon," countered Kelly.

Kelly motioned to Fischer and Grace to step away from the prisoners. They all huddled in the corner of the barn and spoke in low hushed tones.

"Fischer, you and Grace take the driver upstairs and question him. I'll keep the Colonel busy. Make sure the Colonel can't hear you. He looks like a scared 17 or 18 year old kid; he's hurt and doesn't know what's going on. Get him to tell you where the gold is and anything else that helps."

"Okay Kelly," Fischer replied as he and Grace cut the driver's ropes, hoisted him up and took him up the ladder to the loft.

Kelly spent the next half hour firing questions at the Colonel who steadfastly stood by his Geneva Convention line. At 1000, three hours later, they all gathered again in the corner.

Softly, Fischer said, "Kelly, I think we got what we wanted. You were right, the kid is scared shitless. But, after we threatened to throw him in a prison with SS guys and leak that he had given us some really good information about the division, we couldn't shut him up. The trucks are at a town called Schirmeck about 65 kilometers from where we bagged them; that's about 40 miles, Kelly. There are about four officers and 50 men there. Also, there are three Tiger tanks, nine trucks and another Kuebelwagen. He thinks the Colonel made some kind of arrangement with the people back at Nancy to send some fuel there, but he's not sure when it will arrive."

"That gives us a time limit. We're gonna need help for this one. Let me do some checking back at the unit before you say anything to anyone."

"Are you thinkin' about going after it?"

"Nothing ventured, nothing gained."

CHAPTER 2

Camp site behind German lines
Near Maziere, France
1900 hours 10 September 1944

Fischer and Grace took the VW Jeep, along with the driver, and headed for the platoon's last position. Kelly took the Colonel in the Jeep and headed for the Division Trains area to see an associate who ran the mobile supply depot for division headquarters. It was 1900 hours and blackout conditions were in force. Kelly signaled a soldier who was hanging around the entrance to the large, olive drab supply tent and asked him to see if Crapgame was inside. If so, could he come out for a minute, Kelly wants to see him. The soldier walked inside.

Five minutes later a slightly overweight staff sergeant emerged from the tent. He was chewing on a toothpick and in a clipped voice with a strong Brooklyn accent said, "If you want somethin', get your ass inside, I don't wait on officers, much less ex-lieutenants. What the hell do you want?"

"Is anyone inside with you?"

"No, what's it to ya?"

"Good, I got a proposition for you, help me with Fritz here, I can't leave him alone."

"What the...hell, he's a kraut?" he stammered.

"I see we can't get anything past you, Crapgame."

Kelly pulled the Colonel out of the Jeep and walked him into the supply tent.

"Sit down on those boxes, Colonel." Without a word he complied.

"Can you untie my hands, the circulation is cut off."

"Wow, he speaks English."

"Yeah, Hustler, I mean Crapgame."

Kelly untied the Colonel's hands and tied the rope around his feet.

"I need an old uniform, from boots to hat, in this guy's size. You got any in the turn-in pile? The only one I had is too small."

"What's this all about, Kelly, what's in it for me?"

"This." Kelly said, handing the gold bar to Crapgame.

"Lead bar, what the hell?"

"Turn it over and look where I scraped the paint off."

Crapgame turned the bar over and his eyes widened and the corners of his mouth turned up in what almost resembled a smile. "Gold!! How many of these you got?"

"Fourteen...hundred...bars." Kelly intentionally drew it out for effect.

"Fourteen hundred bars?" The toothpick dropped out of his mouth to the dirt floor.

"Take anything you want, uniforms, booze, whatever." Crapgame was visibly excited as he picked up the field phone and cranked the handle. "Izzy, get me a price for gold on the Swiss exchange."

Kelly pulled a uniform out of a pile in the corner and handed it to the Colonel. "Put this on, I want the uniform back 'cause I think the one from the barn is too small for you."

"I think you are right, what are you planning?" asked the Colonel.

"None of your business, now get dressed."

The phone rang and Crapgame excitedly picked it up. "Yeah Izzy? Thirty five...just curious. I got some extra stuff here that I might have melted down." He hung up the phone, put the bar on a scale and began furiously writing. He mumbled incoherently as he figured.

Kelly re-tied the Colonel's feet after he had finished dressing. He looked precisely like a private from the 35th Infantry Division. Kelly folded the Colonel's uniform, pulled out his papers, and wallet and put them in a nearby box.

"Now Colonel, you are a captured enemy agent, in an American uniform with papers from the Das Reich Panzer Division." The Colonel went pale as he realized what would happen if he were caught. Kelly and that uniform were the only things that would keep him from being shot as an enemy agent. Kelly half smiled, "I would advise you to cooperate with us fully or it's over for you. Verstehen Sie?"

"I fully understand Private Kelly, I completely understand."

"Nine million, five hundred thirty-five thousand dollars, Kelly, you're beautiful. What do you need and what's my cut?" Crapgame quickly responded.

Kelly rolled his eyes and shook his head before he answered. "Fill this wish list and you keep the gold bar. What's that worth?"

"About fourteen thousand dollars; what's the split when you get the other bars?"

"An equal share for anyone who makes it to the gold."

"I think a sharp business mind is essential on an enterprise such as this, besides Switzerland is only a hundred miles away, and we don't need anybody taking a wrong turn."

"Are you sure you want to go along, fourteen grand is a nice sum for letting go of some stuff that isn't even yours."

Crapgame thought for a minute before he said, "It looks like the difference between fourteen thousand and maybe half a million if you keep the unit small."

"It looks like fifteen people if you go."

Crap game began to figure again.

"You could use some tank support." The new voice came from behind some boxes stacked at the back of the tent. Kelly swung around and in the dim light he was able to make out a tall, thin buck sergeant with long hair and a scruffy beard. He was wearing a .45 on his right hip. A young girl peered out from behind the boxes next him, buttoning up her blouse.

"Who the hell are you?"

"Oddball, everybody calls him Oddball, he's part of the 737th Tank Battalion that's attached to us."

"We are resting at the moment and repairing our vehicles, preparing for the upcoming offensive that our glorious leader has planned. He fucked up the first try north of Nancy so they gave it to the 80th Division. Now he is going to try to cross the river to the south of Nancy. Luckily the 4th Armored is putting together a Combat Command B, I think it is, and they are going to help us. We definitely need help."

"How many tanks have you got?"

"Two, all ready to go on a five hour notice, but they look like it would take weeks to get them in shape. We keep them that way so nobody pesters us to go fight, not just yet anyway."

"Kelly, I made a slight mistake on the numbers. It's nineteen million, five hundred thirty-five thousand. I'm definitely going along."

"We could become a primo fighting force for a share of that."

"How many men have you got?"

"Ten, two crews of five."

"Crapgame, do we have any maps of this area that go to the German border?"

"I don't, but I'll get some."

"I've got one out in my tank; it'll take me ten minutes to get it."

"Colonel, this is your chance to save your ass."

"I'm listening." He was now "all ears."

"Did you arrange for gas to be delivered to your convoy?" He asked the German.

"Not quite, the General in Nancy said he would send benzene to us when he could. We should not expect it before the 13th, because all his trucks were tied up in the redeployment along the Meurthe to meet the Allied advance. He is expecting the Allies to attack on the 12th or 13th. His trucks would not leave before the night of the 13th and arrive the early morning of the 14th. That was the best he could do. He expects to delay with a fighting retreat."

"Is your convoy going to wait that long for fuel?"

"I don't know, I left the evening of the seventh and arrived in Nancy on the morning of the eighth. We spent all day requesting the fuel and ironing out the details. I left the evening of the ninth but, sadly, you caught me and now have me at your disposal. I would say Sturm-bahnfuehrer Zentgraf will start looking for fuel tomorrow. He will have given up on me."

"Will he start looking tomorrow morning or tomorrow night?"

"He will have to wait for dark; your Air Force makes it very dangerous to travel during the day.

Just then Oddball arrived with the map. He spread it out on the field desk that was Crapgame's domain. Kelly and Oddball studied the map for a full five minutes before Kelly asked. "Can you be in Avricourt between midnight and 0300 on the 14th?"

"If we aren't there, it's 'cause we're dead."

"I'll take you at your word. We will leave Avricourt at 0300 with or without you."

"Oh...Oh yeah...Understood!" Oddball's mind was already on spending the money as far as Kelly could tell.

"Come on Colonel, do I have to tie you up again?"

"No Kelly, I won't leave you unless I become suicidal, which is highly unlikely."

"Crapgame, take care of the Colonel's uniform, it's the only thing between him and a firing squad."

"Right, Kelly." Crapgame was already working on the list Kelly had given him. There were only a few hours to get everything together.

Oddball questioned Crapgame as Kelly and the

Colonel left the tent. "What's that guy Kelly's story? He seems to be more than your average dogface Private."

"He used to be a Lieutenant with the 90th Infantry Division. A couple of companies got cut off because the Battalion CO screwed up. Kelly was with one of the cut off companies and was the only officer to get out. He got out to get ammo and bring it back to the companies that were cut off. The Battalion CO wouldn't let him go back. Both companies got wiped out. They needed someone to blame, besides themselves, so why not a Lieutenant? They demoted him and kicked him out of the Division, he eventually landed here."

"How come he got out in one piece?"

"Don't know, ask him, or Simmons, he comes in here just about every day from the 137th Infantry. He was in the 90th, knows the whole story."

"I'll talk to him tomorrow. I'd like to know what we're getting into. I don't trust officers."

"Neither does he."

CHAPTER 3

Behind German Lines
1 mile east of Bayon, France
2245 hours, 10 September 1944

Kelly backed the Jeep into the trees in the defense perimeter of the Recon Platoon. They had taken up this position on the banks of the Moselle River in the early hours of yesterday morning. Big Joe, the Platoon Leader, had sent Kelly, Fischer and Grace further forward to capture a prisoner to interrogate. He walked the prisoner over to the small barn nearby where Big Joe had set up the small command post.

He carefully knocked on the door and whispered, "It's Kelly, Big Joe."

"Get in here Kelly!" Big Joe boomed as Kelly walked into the dark barn with the Colonel. When he shut the door Little Joe, the radio operator, turned up the kerosene lamp.

"Who the hell is this? I thought you had some goose stepping SS guy and you brought me some 35 year old American private, what the hell…"

Kelly interrupted, "Big Joe, this *is* the SS Colonel we captured and he is very cooperative. He realizes that if we turn him over to S-2 they will get what information they can out of him and then shoot him as a spy."

"Got it all figured out, have you? What'd he tell you?"

Kelly spent the next 5 minutes telling Big Joe about the gold convoy and what he had arranged with Crapgame. Big Joe's response was expected.

"We turn him over to S-2 and get on with our business. Little Joe, you forget what you just heard-a few bucks worth of gold won't do anybody any good if they're dead."

"Joe, over nineteen million dollars isn't a few bucks; it works out to about a million dollars apiece. I'm going after it and taking anybody with me that wants to go."

"You do and you'll be a deserter."

"How's that Joe, do people desert by going 40 miles behind German lines with a couple of Sherman tanks? We'll be lucky if they don't give us medals."

"These guys have been at the front of this division since we landed at Omaha Beach. We have been the point platoon for the entire fucking division. The rear echelon units get to rest behind the lines until a big city is taken. Then they get to spend a couple of days being heroes to all the broads in town. We get to go look for the enemy, most of the time we are behind German lines. Now you want to go further behind the lines! You're nuts, Kelly, none of these guys will go with you."

"They should at least be given a chance to say no."

"This isn't a democracy, Kelly; we follow orders, without question."

"Just like the Germans? Captain Maitland spends most of his time looting what the Germans have left behind, and just because he's a captain he gets away with it. It's our turn now."

Big Joe was beaten and he knew it. Arguing with Kelly was useless. Big Joe was the platoon leader and had been since Lieutenant Connors had been killed at Le Mans on the 17th of August, almost a month ago. Maitland had made no move to replace him. Joe was getting the job done, keeping the S-2 happy with the intelligence he was gathering. He had only lost two men, both killed, since Connors bought it. He was in the middle and finding it increasingly difficult to do what the Battalion S-2 wanted him to do and still keep his men alive. Berlin was a long way off and the German Army that was in front of them had a lot of fight left in it.

Kelly took the next hour explaining his plan to the entire platoon. Most of them wanted Big Joe to lead them because, after all, they were unsure of Kelly. But if it comes down to it, they would go with Kelly leading.

Kelly put it to him, "Big Joe, they are all for it. They want you to lead them. I know you're a career soldier and this wouldn't be good for your career. But, the rest of these guys are in this for the duration, plus six months, and this pot at the end of the rainbow looks a hell of a lot better than the fifty bucks a month we are making now."

"Yeah, Big Joe, there is also the cold K rations to eat and sleeping in the woods on the ground is a real kick. Kelly has even got us armor support," spouted Little Joe.

"What armor...who's in charge?"

"Two Sherman Tanks from the 737th, the guy in charge is called Oddball."

"Oddball, he's a freak, nobody knows where he is half the time. He'll show up only if his stuff is operational and it doesn't look like it is. What about Maitland?"

"Maitland doesn't know where we are most of the time. He has his nose up the General's ass, day and night. I can make reports to the S-2 on the way so no one will be the wiser," Little Joe said, getting a little excited.

Big Joe looked around at the guys in the barn and asked, "What do you think, Corporal?"

"I'm afraid I have to go along with it, Joe."

"Mitchell..."

"I'm in."

"Petuko?...Barbara?...Jonesey?...Gutowski?"

All nodded and Babra spoke up. "Babra, my name is Babra, Joe."

"Right...Babra"

"Cowboy?"

"I reckon I'm for it, Joe."

"Me too, Joe." Willard, the last man in the barn, sealed the deal.

"It looks like I'm alone if I don't go with you nuts." He managed a half smile, better than he had been able to do in the last two years.

All the men in the barn breathed a sigh of relief, Joe was gonna lead them. Then, Kelly and Joe went over the map they had and discussed it in detail.

"What's the scuttlebutt on when Combat Command B jumps off?"

"I heard it was at dawn tomorrow. Radio traffic has gone to almost nil in the last hour."

"Keep listening, Little Joe, let me know if there is any change."

"Will do, Joe."

"It looks like we have about ten or twelve hours to get this thing ready, because obviously, we have to move ahead of the advance. Kelly, where did you cross the river last night?"

"Here at Flavigny, but I don't think that's possible now. The Germans have strong points built up at likely crossings and it will be too difficult to break out. But, they can't cover the entire line. There are plenty of holes in their defenses and they have pulled a lot of troops out of the Moselle line in order to reposition them in the Meurthe Line. I'm pretty sure that the crossing we used is blocked by now."

"What about here, Kelly? Big Joe was pointing to an area just north of Bayon, just before the river forked.

"Yeah Joe, that's right where an artillery barrage dammed up the canal. The river is fordable by Jeep. Then it's a clear shot to the Meurthe. I'm going to get the supplies from Crapgame."

"Take both M3s. Is Crapgame coming?"

"Yeah, he turned down the gold bar right up front." The smirk on Kelly's face said volumes.

"Kelly, take Fischer, Grace and Gutowski with ya."

"You heard him guys, let's go."

They drove the Halftracks to the Division Trains Area and in two hours' time they had finished loading the equipment that Kelly had outlined. Crapgame had been able to get the 100 Jerry cans of gasoline delivered. It cost him a case of scotch, but in view of the mission it was scotch well spent.

They arrived at the Recon platoon position at 0400. Everyone pitched in and they quickly stowed and tied down the 100 jerry cans of gasoline in the two M-3 Halftracks. Cowboy and Willard took the Halftrack mounted with a .50 caliber machine gun. Willard stowed the two bazookas and 18 rounds of ammunition in six cloth bags in the cab. Penn and Petuko, with his BAR weapon, would ride in the back with Penn on the .50 cal. Kelly and Grace would be in the second M-3 with Gutowski, Jonesey and Crapgame in the back to guard the SS Colonel and provide covering fire. Big Joe and Little Joe would be in the first Jeep with Fischer, Babra in the second Jeep and Mitchell and Corporal Job manned the third Jeep. Each man in the platoon got a Thompson submachine gun with three pouches of five, thirty round clips each, rations for six days and six grenades. Little Joe had the pack radio in the Jeep and each vehicle had a walkie talkie. They left their fourth Jeep behind. Big Joe hadn't seen the right front fender, much to Kelly's relief. They left the German Kuebelwagen near the barn.

The column pulled into position an hour before daybreak and joined CCB, which was about a mile from crossing the Moselle River. The artillery prep began at exactly zero four thirty and the first elements of CCB crossed the canal which Kelly and the other recon elements had used for the last three days. The canal was dried up because of shell craters from earlier bombardments. It had created dams about 200 meters apart, leaving the area in between virtually dry. They forded the Moselle between Bayon and Lorey per Recon's instructions. They quickly widened the gap, cleaned out the German resistance on their flanks, and moved forward until they dug in for the night very close to where the Recon Platoon had camped for two days near Bayon.

At 1900 Kelly parked his Halftrack in the woods

between the small village of Charmois and Damele-vieres. The rest of the vehicles were soon hidden in the copse of trees away from prying eyes. CCB had been bashing the German front lines all day until they dug in at last light. CCB's artillery was being moved up to the new position and by 0100 would be ready for fire missions. Big Joe sensed that Crapgame wouldn't be able to sleep, so he detailed him to stay awake and keep watch. For most soldiers, waiting for the kickoff was a time to write letters and try to calm their nerves. This was true for Crapgame and the SS Colonel who both had spent most of their time in the rear. But little would be expected of either of them tomorrow. The surviving battle hardened men of the recon platoon grabbed any rest when they could, for as long as they could. Crap-game and the SS Colonel, both alert on sentry duty, were the only ones that were awake. The SS Colonel had resigned himself to the fact that his future lay with these American soldiers.

At 0330 everybody was awake and Big Joe whispered his briefing to the platoon for the vehicle line up for the Meurthe River crossing.

"Kelly, you and Grace lead and keep Gutowski, Jonesey, Crapgame and the kraut Colonel in the back. Hustler, shoot him if he tries to escape. I'll be right be-hind you with Little Joe. Fischer, you and Babra are be-hind me. Cowboy, you and Willard are fourth with Penn and Petuko in the back. Corporal, you and Mitchell bring up the rear. Everybody rides on the next guy's bumper. The artillery boys are going to start a rolling barrage beginning 1000 meters south of wV006960 to be delivered at 0355. That's 22 minutes from now. We move up to that group of buildings at the end of this road and wait. Keep the engines running, and Kelly, you take off up that railroad track when the first rounds impact. Any questions? Hmmm. Good, give me that hand set, Little Joe."

"Sure, Arty is on the other end, Joe, but how are you going to get a fire mission without Battalion's approval?"

"Let me worry about that, get movin'!"

Everybody ran to their vehicles, and within three minutes slowly started to move to the jump off point. Big Joe called the Artillery Fire Control Center.

"Nuptial Bravo Roger Two Sugar this is Lucky Recon Six, Fire Mission Over."

"Lucky Recon Six this is Nuptial Bravo Roger Two Sugar Go."

"Rolling barrage Two Rounds Wide. Start Point Four Thousand Meters South of Map Reference Whiskey Victor Zero Zero, Six Nine Six Zero, to Four Thousand Meters North Azimuth Zero One Five Degrees. Start Zero Three Five Five Over."

"Roger Lucky Recon Six, Whiskey Victor Zero Zero, Six Niner Six Zero, Four Thousand Meters South to Four Thousand Meters North, Zero One Five Degrees, Impact Zero Three Five Five Hours Out."

"Isn't Lucky Six Patton's call sign?" Little Joe's eyes were wide.

"Can you think of a better way to get artillery fire four miles north of CCB's position? They didn't even ask us to authenticate, definitely a mistake on their part, good for us."

Kelly stopped at the jump off point at 0350. They were at the junction of the railroad tracks that ran north into Damelevieres and the road that ran into the village of Charmois off to their left. As is usual with soldiers before jumping off on an operation, everyone was tight as a bow string.

CHAPTER 4

Breakout Position
1500 Meters South of Damelevieres
0354 hours 12 September 1944

KRUMP, KRUMP, the first two 105 artillery rounds impacted. Each one was a hemispherical shower of burning white phosphorus, impossible to miss in the darkness. Kelly drove forward on the railroad bed with the column bumper to bumper right behind him. They were engulfed in the smoke left by the initial rounds when the next rounds impacted at Kelly's eleven and one o'clock positions, about 40 meters out on the left front and 100 meters on the right. He knew that the least danger of shrapnel was at the rear of the explosion, so he adjusted his course to stay well to the rear of each impact. Two Jeeps were sandwiched between the two Halftracks. Cowboy, in the second Halftrack, was in the worst position. He had to concentrate on the two Jeeps and also gauge the effect of the artillery. Any short rounds would land in his lap. Kelly was gaining ever so slightly on the exploding rounds. Penn opened up with the .50 Cal on two Germans that had started to crawl out of their slit trenches on Cowboy's left. Seconds later Petuko began firing on three Germans in a ditch beside the railroad right of way. He continued to fire to keep their heads down until Corporal Job and Mitchell, bringing up the rear, opened up with their Thompsons.

Each of the 105 rounds were impacting about 75 meters in front of the last explosion, giving an overlapping pattern. The noise was thunderous and the debris thrown up by each explosion was falling on the racing vehicles. Kelly was now approximately 75 meters from the explosion to his left front and less than 100 meters from the explosion to his right front. All seemed to be going well. Suddenly, Kelly spotted a German near a tree to his left front. "Grace, one o'clock by the tree!" he shouted.

Grace was standing in the cab. He swung around and sprayed a clip in the direction of the tree, but the German had ducked behind the large oak. While Grace was ramming another clip into his Thompson, the German jumped out from his cover. Gutowski took him down with a six round burst before his bolt stayed back on an empty magazine. By this time Grace had reloaded and sent a five round burst in that general direction.

A minute later the explosion that Kelly was expecting 100 meters to his right front exploded in the trees approximately 50 meters to the right of Big Joe's Jeep. Shrapnel hit the side of the Jeep and Little Joe's right thigh near the knee.

"I'm hit, Joe!" he shouted!

Big Joe looked over at him and could see his torn pants about three inches above the knee. "How bad?"

"Don't know yet."

"Keep a lookout, it looks like a short round," he yelled, hoping that a tank or antitank gun hadn't zeroed in on them.

Willard had seen the round impact and the debris that hit the Jeep and shouted, "I think Big Joe's been hit!"

"How bad?"

"Don't know. I'll try to cover them."

The railroad bed began curving to the right. Kelly was glad to see the overpass over the road was still intact. The round to Kelly's left front was about 50 meters away. The next round was less than 40 meters to Kelly's right front and had they not been behind the explosion they would have had a lot of shrapnel to contend with. Kelly slowed and Big Joe's Jeep hit the back end of Kelly's vehicle. Big Joe hadn't anticipated the slow down because the exploding rounds to the right were hidden by the bulk of the Halftrack in front. Fischer had seen the explosion and throttled back before Kelly did. Cowboy anticipated it, but Corporeal Job hit the back of Cowboy's Track. Kelly continued driving on the railroad tracks which now began to curve to the left. Kelly was only about 35 meters from the round on the right front when it exploded. Again, he had stayed to the rear of the impact where the blast was weakest. The next round was off to the left front about 75 meters. The Tracks had exited the corridor of artillery fire and Kelly slammed his foot to the floor as did all the other vehicles and they shot forward as fast as possible. Everyone was suffering from the bone jarring thumping caused by driving at 30 miles an hour on the railroad ties. They crossed the last overpass that spanned the tracks over the D1 Highway. Now this was a race to the river; speed and the guns on board were their only cover.

The 105 shells had been on track landing at 50-75 meters in front of Kelly's position when he passed the last house on that side of town. He was hoping against hope that the bridge across the Meurthe was still intact. All their guns were suppressing fire from the buildings on both sides of the railroad. Kelly knew that the bridge was less than half a football field ahead. He was already at 30 miles per hour, as much as could be expected on this very bumpy surface and the bridge was about 30 seconds ahead. Everyone had stopped firing as soon as they passed the last buildings. The railroad tracks were now continuing their long sweeping left turn that had started just before reaching the edge of town. They were headed out of the artillery corridor as fast as possible on the railroad bed when the last rounds of the rolling barrage exploded at Kelly's four o'clock position.

Suddenly they began taking fire from the trees to the left and right; all the guns in the convoy began to suppress it with everything they had. Kelly started across the bridge when he spotted a German Halftrack on the main tracks to their right before this spur line intersected. The driver stopped suddenly when he spotted the American convoy. The machine gunner in the cab swung his post-mounted MG-42 machine gun towards Kelly's Halftrack. The six German soldiers in the rear were scrambling to get a clear shot.

Without warning a series of German 88 artillery rounds hit in the area just to the right of the tracks intersection where Kelly was headed. One of the rounds impacted five feet from the rear of the German Halftrack. It lifted the rear of the vehicle six or seven feet off the ground sending the soldiers in the back flying. All of them hit the ground like rag dolls, two of them were on fire. Kelly took a dirt road to his left leaving the grizzly scene behind. He could see the assistant driver hanging out the window on the right side, bleeding from the nose, mouth and ears. If he wasn't dead, he probably wished he was. Each vehicle followed Kelly's lead as they sped towards the D110 highway that crossed the extensive switching yards. Everyone was happy to leave the railroad tracks. When they crossed the bridge Gutowski could see the machine gunner in the cab. He was almost cut in half. *Better you than me.*

The rest of the column sped across the bridge and followed Kelly a short distance on the main road that led out of town. There were six Germans around a parked truck near the crossroads and they scattered as Gutowski and Jonesey opened fire. Cowboy swerved his vehicle to ram the truck at the side of the road and Penn chopped it up with the .50 cal. Kelly turned onto a dirt road to his right as he knew from the sound that they had been pinpointed by German Artillery Spotters, probably from the village. The last two barrages had been compliments of those Spotters. *Time to get off the road and into the woods.* The road went through the forest. He kept driving, picking up familiar terrain features that he, Fischer, and Grace had used the other night when they caught the SS Colonel. Kelly yelled at Crapgame as they drove. "Crapgame, did everybody make it okay?"

"Yeah, Kelly, everybody is still there." He said looking back.

20 minutes later Kelly stopped on a farm road and signaled the others to hold up.

Grace asked him, "Isn't this where we dumped the guy from that SS Colonel's Jeep?"

"Yeah it is. Why don't you go back and see if he's still where you left him."

"Why?"

"If he's still there we'll know they haven't missed the Colonel yet."

"Good thinkin'." Grace walked back into the woods.

"You okay, Big Joe?" He asked in a low calm voice.

"Little Joe's been hit in the leg."

"Bad?"

"I've got it bandaged, but he says it burns like hell, small pieces of shrapnel, maybe even rocks. I won't know until we stop long enough for someone to take a look."

"I'll see if Penn can take a look."

"Thanks, Kelly."

Kelly went back to Cowboy's Halftrack.

"Penn, go take a look at Little Joe- he caught one in the leg."

"Will do." Penn walked to Big Joe's Jeep and began taking the field dressing off Little Joe's leg.

Kelly went to Job and Fischer's vehicles. No casualties, that was a plus. As he walked past Big Joe's Jeep, Joe said, "Where to from here?"

"We cross the hardball ahead and then drive about six miles cross country to a little village called Gellenoncourt. Just to the east of there we look for a place to hold up for the day. We can't travel during the day. Our own damned Airforce will chop us to pieces. Most of this is open country, no place to hide. And with the 4th Armored and the 35th attacking Nancy, the Air Force boys will be just waiting for anything moving in this area."

"It's already too light for my taste. Let's get moving!"

"Whatever you say, Joe"

Grace came running from the woods and jumped on Kelly's Halftrack.

"The body's gone, I guess they know the Colonel is missing," Grace said, breathing hard from the run in the woods.

"Can't be helped, keep an eye out."

It was just after sunrise before they found a hiding place about three miles east of Gellenoncourt. They were able to drive through a plowed field using the recently plowed rows to hide their tracks into the trees. Each vehicle was well hidden, about 50 feet into the forest. It was just in time, too. At about 0830 a flight of Thunderbolts flew over the area looking for targets of opportunity. They would be able to rest here for the day and take care of the vehicles and Little Joe's leg.

"Damn, Penn that hurts like hell!"

"Sit still. Little Joe, I'm workin' here."

"It's my leg you're working on...what's that?"

"That my friend, is a piece of good old US Steel, probably from Pittsburgh. Looks like part of a 105 shell. Now, hold still, there's more."

"How much more?"

"You don't want to know. Now do as I say or I'll leave that shit in your leg and when it infects the doctors will remove it *and* your goddamned leg."

"Okay, okay, but be gentle. I'm very delicate."

"Yeah, yeah."

Penn continued to poke around the wounds on Little Joe's leg. Corporal Job walked up to the Jeep carrying a bag and an ammo box and asked, "how many clips you need Penn?"

"Two ought to do it and give me 90 rounds loose. Little Joe can load my empty clips while I save his leg."

"Why do I have to load your clips?"

"Doctor's bill, buddy"

"How 'bout you, Little Joe?"

"60 rounds loose, I didn't do a lot of shootin' after that shit nearly took my leg off."

The Corporal got eight 20 round boxes and two new clips out of the bag.

"How's the leg lookin'?" Corporal Job asked as he leaned over Penn's shoulder for a closer look. Penn was pulling a 4 inch long wooden splinter out of the leg.

"Ow, damn you, Penn, what is that?"

"Looks like a huge splinter," observed Job.

"Very good, Corporal, I think there is a rock left in there. You're gonna' be sore for a long time, Little Joe."

"I would say so," Job quipped as he went to Kelly's Track to pass out more ammunition.

Kelly and Big Joe were looking over the map while Corporal Job questioned Gutowski, Jonesey and Crapgame.

"How many clips Gutowski?"

"I'm empty, Corporal, all fifteen clips."

"You're trigger-happy Gutowski, take it easy," Job said, stacking fifteen boxes of ammo by Gutowski. He rapped Gutowski hard on the shoulder as he said, "you only get 10 clips worth, take it easy…I mean it!"

"Will do, Corporal." Gutowski said, somewhat sheepishly.

"60 for me, Corporal." Jonesey didn't look up from the K-ration box that he was opening.

"You need any clips?"

"No, I got all mine off the floor of the Track."

"Crapgame?"

"One box 'ill do 'cause I was watching the Kraut most of the time."

Job handed him a box without any comment. He walked over to Cowboy's Halftrack.

"Cowboy, Willard, how about you?"

"About 120 rounds, I reckon."

"Looks like 60 for me. I was doing all the shootin'. I had to use Cowboy's Thompson when mine jammed. I figured things were too exciting to stop shootin' and clear a jam."

"Yeah, Willard done good, Corporal, he nailed several of 'em."

Job put 9 boxes between them. Petuko was sitting up against the front tire.

"Petuko, BAR Ammo?"

"All twelve clips worth, I only have one left."

"Here's twelve boxes, reload the magazines you

have and another 12 boxes to load the twelve magazines that are in the back of Kelly's Track. Get a carrier while you're at it. What about ammo for the .50?"

"Penn's got two boxes, he used up two belts. The other box of two is just in case."

Job walked over to the command Jeep where Penn was just finishing bandaging Little Joe's leg. "How's he doing?"

"He'll live if he keeps it clean; if he doesn't, it'll kill him."

"Thanks for that, Penn, it would make your day, wouldn't it?"

"You said it, I didn't."

"Cut it out, you two...Little Joe, take these empty Thompson clips and this ammo and load em up. I'll bring you some more ammo if you need it."

"I'm a radio operator, why do I have to load clips."

"You're the only one who doesn't have anything to do but bitch and because I said so."

"Thanks, Corporal." Little Joe's voice dripped with sarcasm.

An hour later, when they had all eaten and were dozing, Fischer stood up and looked around.

"What is it?" Kelly asked.

"Sounds like an engine, maybe a plane over there." He pointed to the southwest.

"Everybody, don't move and keep down. It's probably one of ours, but nobody knows we're here except the Kraut. Where is the Kraut?"

"Here, Sergeant, don't worry, I don't want to get shot by one of yours or one of mine either." He was sitting up against the front wheel of Kelly's Halftrack.

The plane got closer and closer until they could see it through the trees. It was about half a mile away, circling near Gellenoncourt to their west.

"He's lookin', keep down and don't move," whispered Joe.

"It looks like he has widened his circle to that other village, Kelly."

"I think you're right, Joe, keep your fingers crossed."

The P-47 made a wide circle and suddenly made a sharp climbing right turn. He rolled out for a gun run on the copse of trees where the column had taken shelter. Then he opened fire.

"Cover!" yelled Big Joe and they all dove to the ground. Trees cracked and limbs fell as the .50 caliber rounds pounded the trees and ground. Suddenly the rounds struck metal and rubber. Joe leaped to his feet as did Kelly. The P-47 had put a three second burst into the trees. The armor piercing rounds had ripped through the side of Cowboy's Halftrack and had destroyed the rear of Big Joe's Jeep. There were several small fires on the ground from the tracer rounds.

"Get those fires out, ASAP!" Joe ordered as he watched the aircraft make a climbing left turn, probably, so he could see if there were any secondary explosions or fires. He leveled off and flew east, probably saddened that his recon by fire hadn't produced any major results.

"Our hero," proclaimed Joe.

"He missed the gas cans and only put a few holes in the left and right side of the Halftrack's bed. It looks like your Jeep got it pretty bad. Little Joe?"

"No, I'm not OK. My leg is killing me and I get the feeling someone has it in for me. Who was that fucker?"

"Never mind, Fischer, you and Barbara move the radio and the rest of the stuff to your Jeep. Everybody... check for damage."

Little Joe hobbled to Fischer's Jeep while Cowboy and Willard inspected their Track. Kelly and Grace gave theirs the once over. They removed the fallen limbs from Job's Jeep and put out the eight small fires that had been started by the tracer rounds. Two of the trees were smoldering 15 feet up.

"Hey Joe, what about these two trees that are smoking?"

"Leave 'em, if our hero comes back he'll know he set this forest on fire. Penn, you and Grace put out fire on my Jeep tire. Trees burn white smoke, rubber burns black smoke."

Penn and Grace doused the smoldering tire with water from a five gallon Jerry can. It was a full two hours before all the work was finished. Big Joe's Jeep was stripped and the gas siphoned into the two other Jeeps. Fischer and Babra moved their equipment to Cowboy's

Track, giving their Jeep to Big Joe. Everybody kicked back until nightfall.

Unbeknownst to Kelly or Big Joe, Combat Command A of the 4th Armored Division was poised to cross the 80th Infantry Division's bridgehead across the Moselle at Dieulouard. CCA planned to knife through Nancy and make it to Chateau Salins by day's end tomorrow, the 13th. This would set them up to turn south to join up with CCB near Arracourt on Sept 14, thereby encircling the 553rd Volksgrenadier Division. The D-2 highway that crossed and recrossed the Marne-Rhine Canal would become their only escape route. CCA would run into elements of the 15th Panzer Division at the canal. The Air Corps will have a field day tomorrow. Kelly and Big Joe's plan was to escape through the lightly defended area before it would become the scene of a major struggle. As if on cue it started to rain at 1000 hours. Everyone took refuge under the Halftracks or in the Jeeps. They would start engines at 1900 hours and start cross country north of the Marne-Rhine Canal. Until then Grace and Crapgame, huddled under their ponchos, were awake. The first watch had begun, it was 1300 hours.

CHAPTER 5

Highway D23
South of Coins Court and Parrot
2249 hours 12 September 1944

The rain had just stopped when the convoy left their camp at 1800 hours. Mitchell was driving the trail Jeep. Penn was on the .50 cal in Cowboy's Track. Kelly was doing the best he could leading the way at night. The waning crescent moon had risen twenty minutes ago and the low cloud cover blocked what little light there was.

The group had covered a little over fifteen miles since they had started. Cross country travel on a moonless night was slow going. They had to circumnavigate what the French called a pond, but it was more like a lake. Kelly stopped about 200 meters before the road that ran between the two tiny villages of Coincourt and Parrot. Kelly and Big Joe had decided to pass midway between the two villages. Corporal Job and Mitchell came up from the rear to scout the road ahead. The convoy was parked on a tractor path between two fields. The grain planted in the northern field was about three and a half, maybe four feet tall; it was ready to harvest according to Cowboy and Willard. The field to the south had been harvested and offered no cover at all. Big Joe stood in front of Kelly's Track with his binoculars.

"It looks like a line of trees up ahead, maybe four trees. I can't make out anything else, Corporal."

"We'll take a look and get back as quick as we can."

"Be careful."

As they drove off down the narrow dirt track, Job said, "Will do, Joe."

Kelly climbed back into the driver's seat. Joe stayed by the right fender of the Track straining to see through the binoculars. Suddenly a machine gun opened up on the Jeep along with other guns from the main road. Seconds later the Jeep veered off to the right and burst into flames.

"Into the wheat field, Kelly!" Joe yelled as he sprinted back to his Jeep.

Kelly gunned the Track and sped into the wheat field. Seconds later Cowboy did the same. Joe jumped into the driver's seat, jammed it into gear and cleared the road

just before the first round from a tank's main gun exploded where Kelly had been parked. Kelly pulled about 100
feet into the field and stopped. Joe drove left until he got
on Cowboy's tracks and followed him till he stopped.

"Fischer, Petuko, grab the bazooka and get over
here. Little Joe, get in the driver's seat and drive until
you find Kelly's tracks and bring Gutowski and Grace
back here."

"On my way, Big Joe!" He turned towards the east
and headed off.

Fischer was carrying the bazooka and three rockets
in a canvas carrier and Petuko carried six rockets in two
canvas bags and his BAR with a twelve magazine belt
around his waist.

"Fischer, you and Petuko get set up on the road, I
think we have a tank coming after us. There were two
MG 34's firing from four or five feet off the ground. It's
probably a Mark VI. Set up for a side shot. Go!"

Without a word they both took off. Joe told Cowboy
to turn left and angle back towards the road, then stop
about 50 meters from the edge of the field. About three
minutes later Little Joe arrived and Joe, Gutowski and
Grace jumped up on the running boards. Cowboy drove
off. In the meantime, Kelly had turned right and driven
50 meters, and then angled back towards the edge of
the field. He shut the Track down when he heard the
Mark VI coming up the tractor path. Kelly and Grace
dismounted the Halftrack and moved toward the path.

Little Joe drove almost to the edge of the field and Big Joe got out.

"Wait here, give me that radio. Is Cowboy on the horn?"

"Yeah Joe, he's listening."

"Cowboy, when I give the word you get onto the road and open up on that tank as soon as Fischer gets a shot."

"Wilco, Joe."

The Mark VI moved up the road until it came to where Kelly had gone in. He didn't dare go into the field after him so he fired a round, straight between the track marks. It impacted about 500 meters away. Petuko took three cardboard tubes out of the carrier and placed them on the ground. He removed the rocket rounds from their tubes. Petuko gently shoved a round into the back of the bazooka tube and wound the wire around the electric terminal. He gave Fischer the customary pat on the helmet and laying prone he set up the BAR on its forward tripod. When the tank was about 40 feet in front of Fischer he fired the first round. It caught the tank in the side armor, just below the middle of the turret. Petuko was loading another rocket as the first round penetrated the 30 mm thick armor plating. It exploded inside the tank, blowing the tank Commander, who was in the opened hatch, a good 20 feet in the air. The driver crawled out of his hatch and was dispatched with a burst of Petuko's BAR. Fischer removed the rocket from the bazooka and put both rounds back in the carrier. Fischer and Petuko picked up their equipment and ran toward Kelly's position. They both had run about 50 feet when the Tiger's ammo and fuel blew. The road was lit up like Times Square. Cowboy met Fischer and Petuko at the edge of the field. Joe had ordered Cowboy out onto the road for Grace to open up on the tank with the .50 cal as a diversion. Fischer's first round kill precluded the need for Cowboy to draw fire while Pettuko reloaded the bazooka.

"Kelly you go down the left, Cowboy you go right and I'm goin' up the middle."

"Good one, Fischer!" Cowboy yelled as he drove past the blazing tank. He knew that he had the light at his back just like the Panzer had experienced the light from the burning Jeep at his back. Penn was raking the area ahead and to the left front with the .50 cal while Cowboy made his way through the plowed field parallel to the tractor path. Kelly, on Cowboy's left rear, was on the other side of the path. Petuko opened up with the BAR as soon as Kelly started his run. Joe was about 30 meters behind them covering their rear.

Bernhard Goetz, a German Wehrmacht Feldwebel from the 15th Panzergrenadier Division, lay in the field barely visible in the flickering light of the burning Jeep and Panzer. Playing dead, he was lying down on the side of the path to avoid the .50 caliber fire Penn was laying down. He watched intently as Cowboy's Track passed. He clutched an MP40 submachine gun, which he had taken from a fallen Fallshirmjaeger. The dead German paratrooper had been incorporated in his unit after his 15th Parachute Regiment had been chopped up in the Bocage during the battle at Mont Castre.

Bernhard rolled to a sitting position in the wink of an eye and sprayed Kelly's Halftrack with his MP40. He didn't see the results of his shot because Crapgame had sent a burst from his Thompson into Bernhard's chest. He died instantly. Grace, standing up in the passenger seat of Kelly's Track, was hit and fell forward. Gutowski pulled Grace to the back of the Halftrack. Jonesey saw what was going on and directed his fire to the right front to cover them while Gutowski took care of Grace. When they stopped at the narrow paved country road thirteen German soldiers were dead and the Mark VI Panzer was still ablaze.

No one celebrated the victory because they all knew they had become complacent. The belief that all the Germans were in the front line was discarded. They were deep in enemy territory. There was no reason to check the bodies of Corporal Job or Mitchell because they were motionless in the burning Jeep. Grace lay dead in the back of Cowboy's Halftrack. Gutowski covered Grace with a blanket. Gutowski and Jonesey hoisted Grace's lifeless body out of the Halftrack and placed it near the burning Jeep. Big Joe lingered for a few minutes near the three soldiers that were his companions at the Utah Beach landing in July, that was less than three months ago.

Cowboy fell into the trail position behind Big Joe, with Kelly still in the lead. The next three miles were very tense, no time to grieve the loss of their companions. That would have to come later. The ever shrinking convoy stopped in a treeline above the small farm road bridge west of Legarde for a break. It was now 0215 and Big Joe was surveying the bridge across the Marne-Rhine canal.

"It looks okay. We'll try to cross after we rest here."

"All together, Joe?"

"Yeah Kelly, I ain't takin' any chances like the last one. We all go at once. If it's an ambush we all go together."

"I agree." Joe handed Kelly his binoculars.

CHAPTER 6

Between US and German Lines
East of Framboise, France
0130 Hours 13 September, 1944

Oddball and Whiskey, the two tank Commanders from the 737th Tank Battalion, had been shadowing the 42nd Armored Cav Squadron that was screening the 4th Armored Division's southern flank. At the town of Gerbeviller on 13 September at 0100 hours, the Cav turned north towards the outskirts of Luneville. Oddball kept on the road to Framboise. Both men had decided to keep the speed to 30 mph to scare any German Infantry into cover, and hopefully to surprise any German armor. If they were lucky, they would be surprised long enough for the two vehicles to get by! It was possible that the Germans would think that they were screening for a much larger force. The German lines here were like a sieve. Not near enough troops to man the front that was at least a half a mile further to the east. The resistance would tighten up as they got closer to the Meurthe River.

"Whiskey, let's go around this next village, they might alert the guys on the bridge."

"Wilco, Oddball."

"Moriarty, go around that village up ahead."

"Whatever you say...boss." Moriarty smirked as he gnawed on his already well chewed cigar. He steered to the right and rode off the road and through some open fields. The ground was hard and flat even after last night's rain, just what the doctor ordered.

"We should be at the bridge anytime now, better load up, Whiskey."

"Wilco, Oddball."

Jesse, the loader, had heard Oddball tell the other Sherman to load, so he had done the same.

"What'd ya put in, Jesse."

"AP Boss, Armor Piercing." Oddball nodded and keyed his mike.

"Whiskey, load High Explosive till we see what's at the bridge."

"Roger." There was no mistaking Whiskey's Texas twang.

"Oddball, you want me to load HE too?"

"No, but keep one handy."

"Okay, here is the long straight stretch, less than a mile to the bridge. There will be a 45 degree turn to the right and the bridge is right there. Turk, keep a sharp eye out."

Oddball looked over his shoulder and keyed the mic. "Whiskey, close it up!"

Oddball had unlocked the .50 cal five minutes ago and swerved it to the left side of the Sherman. Whiskey had done the same except his gun was covering the right side. Oddball took his Thompson out of its bracket, he flipped the safety off. Seconds later the road curved to the right and they were on the bridge approach. There was a wooden barricade across the road. The two guards on the bridge jumped to the side of the road as Oddball's Tank sliced through the wooden gate. Splinters flew onto the turret forcing Oddball to duck inside.

Whiskey had rotated his turret 180 degrees during the run in. As his Sherman cleared the bridge Whiskey yelled, "fire!"

Wally pressed the foot firing switch and the round was on its way with a deafening roar and a cloud of smoke.

"Load one, Murph!"

"Keep their heads down, Wally!"

Murph had already ejected the spent shell and rammed another one into the breech. In the five seconds since he fired Wally had adjusted the gun elevation.

When he felt Murph's tap on his shoulder he pressed the foot switch again.

Murph had another round in the breech when Whiskey yelled, "Cease fire!"

"Moriarty, the road slowly curves to the left after that farm house on the right. We leave the road in the middle of the curve and go cross country. There is a railroad track after you leave the road."

"Got it, Chief." Moriarty's voice cracked in Oddball's headset.

Moriarty slowed down to 20 mph and made a slow 90 degree turn to the right. He slowed down further for the ditches on each side of the railroad bed. Suddenly Oddball caught movement out of the corner of his eye.

"Hit it, Moriarty, Turk, target right." Turk was already cranking the turret around as Moriarty poured the coals to it. It was a Mark VI about 200 meters down the track. The Panzer fired and the shell screamed past the rear of Oddball's tank. Turk had the turret of the Mark VI in his sights. He pressed the footswitch and the round struck the turret of the enemy tank.

"Get us outta here, Moriarty, Turk, see if you can get a deflection shot."

"I'm workin' on it." Turk fired and a split second later, the round exploded on the Mark VI's turret. Turk's shot hit to the left of the main gun. They picked up speed and Oddball held his breath as Whiskey's tank leaped forward just as he fired. The Mark VI fired and the round went behind Whiskey. The Panzer began to move forward as Whiskey loaded another round and prepared a side shot.

"I'll tell you when to fire, Wally."

"Gotcha, Whiskey."

Whiskey was contemplating whether to go for the track drive wheel or a hull side shot and possibly send the occupants to Valhalla.

"Go for the hull side shot, Wally, fire when ready."

Wally made last minute adjustments to the elevation. He pressed the foot switch when the side was visible. The round found the target and bore through the 30 mm armor on the hull side before it exploded inside the tank. Whiskey's tank was just going into the apple orchard when the Tiger's ammo and fuel blew. It lit up the entire railyard. Once inside the trees, Moriarty slowed down and Whiskey's driver, Barney, followed suit. Nobody remembered Barney's real name so they started calling him Barney after the race car driver, Barney Oldfield. Barney had a tendency to drive too fast.

"One tense situation, Whiskey, everything okay?"

"Yeah, Oddball, might have to clean my pants when we get to a river."

"Know what you mean, that fucker came out of nowhere."

"Oddball, we *are* behind German lines, it's to be expected. Hope that's the last one for tonight." Whiskey made no attempt to hide the sarcasm.

Oddball kept to the forest paths that were vaguely apparent in the waning crescent moonlight. They heard trucks on the highway when they pulled up at the edge of the trees, outside the village of Thiebaumenil. It was almost 0200 before they could cross the highway and continue. The trucks were spread out about 200 meters apart and headed for Luneville.

Both tanks skirted the tiny village of Manonviller on the Rue de la Gare or the D161 if you're looking at the map. No traffic there, but it was a 45 minute wait before they could cross the Embermenil-Veho road. Truck after truck filled with troops went by. They were spaced 200 meters apart and were headed for either Nancy or the Marne-Rhine Canal. The convoys were traveling with blackout lights. It only took about ten minutes for both tanks to drive between the stops, but waiting for the convoys made each leg of the journey take 30-45 minutes. There was a big push on with lots of troops heading towards Nancy, but beyond that, it was anybody's guess as to exactly what the Germans were thinking.

The morning sun was just peeking over the horizon when Oddball's merry band pulled into a patch of moderately dense forest and they shut the vehicles down. The rain clouds had disappeared during the night and it promised to be a clear day. Lorraine's population had been under German rule from 1870 to 1918, then France reclaimed the area after WWI as part of the Armistice. The people were mostly ethnic Germans, therefore sympathized with Nazi Germany. It was likely that a farmer in this area would report two Sherman Tanks to the German authorities. They had to move at night for the same reason the Germans moved at night, because the US Army Air Corps couldn't tell friend from foe at 300 miles an hour.

Oddball and Whiskey were standing by a tree at the edge of the forest, both looking intently through their binoculars at the small town of Avricourt.

"Looks like the Jerrys are all over that place, Whiskey."

"Yep, looks like a three or four road junction, plus the railroad. They will fight for this place and fight hard."

"Hopefully, they will be transporting men and equipment on the railroad and won't notice us when we go around the town."

"That'd be the smart move, and that bunch usually makes the smart move."

"Moriarty and Rocky are trying to raise Kelly on the radio."

"Chuck is trying too. But they hadn't had any luck when I left."

"I don't think they made it here yet, but it's possible. Kelly had said the night of the fourteenth, that's tomorrow."

"Maybe, Oddball, I'd hate to be out here all by our lonesome. Not too many friendly faces around, if you know what I mean."

"You're right Whiskey...you're right."

* * *

Edge of Forest
1.5 Miles NW of Lagarde
0225 Hours 13 September 1944

While Oddball and Whiskey were stopping at every major north-south road waiting for convoys of German troops to pass, Kelly's two Halftracks and one remaining Jeep left the cover of the forest headed for the only bridge where the D89 highway crossed the Marne-Rhine Canal for miles. There were two sentries on duty, but no roadblock. Cowboy was in the lead with Fischer on the .50 cal and Petuko with his BAR. Joe was tail end Charlie. They sped down the narrow farm road towards the main road and the bridge. They had learned with their three months' combat experience that speed and surprise were the answers to most problems, as long as you were the one speeding and they were the ones surprised.

The two Germans privates on the road were foreign conscripts. Their NCO was in the town with several German soldiers, but most of the small guard unit consisted of Poles who were forcibly conscripted into the

Wehrmacht. They watched in awe as Cowboy's Halftrack approached. One of them realized the vehicles were American, dropped his rifle, and threw up his hands. The other followed suit very quickly. Cowboy was more than surprised and Willard motioned them aside with his Thompson. Both men moved to the right side of the vehicle, Cowboy gunned the engine, and started across the bridge. The two Poles began shouting and waving their arms and dove off the road into the ditch! Cowboy's front wheels were less than half way across the bridge when there was an explosion to his left rear. Willard ducked, as did Petuko. Fischer and Babra were thrown back into the bed of the Halftrack by the explosion. Shrapnel came up through the floor and punctured about twenty Jerry cans. Very quickly there was gasoline everywhere. Fischer picked himself up out of a puddle created by three leaking cans next to him.

"Get out before she blows!" yelled Willard as he jumped off the left side of the stricken vehicle. Petuko grabbed Fischer, who was visibly shaken.

"You all right?"

"I think so. I'm soaked with gasoline, what happened?"

"Jump off the left side before this thing blows," yelled Petuko!

Cowboy had gunned the engine and turned the wheel to the right. The right track was digging in, but the left track was lying on the bridge and the drive wheels were spinning. The vehicle crawled forward veering right.

"You all right Cowboy?" Willard yelled.

"Yeah...I think."

Suddenly the gasoline ignited and the flames leaped five feet high in the back.

"Get out Cowboy...Get out now!" Willard yelled.

"That's what I'm a-thinkin'." Cowboy's voice was strained. He grabbed his Thompson and jumped clear of the burning Halftrack.

As soon as he was out, Kelly rammed the now engulfed Track and pushed it over the side of the bridge and into the water. He floored it and leaped across the rest of the bridge to the road beyond. The gasoline was burning on top of the water as the Halftrack rolled over on its side and sank with only the burning gasoline to mark its watery grave.

"Get your asses on Kelly's Track...Now!" Joe's voice was urgent as he had spotted a set of headlights about halfway between the village and their position on the bridge. Fischer, Petuko, Babra, Willard and Cowboy ran to Kelly's vehicle. With Gutowski and Jonesey's help they climbed aboard. Big Joe stopped on the bridge as Kelly took off across the open field on the other side of the road. Joe flipped the safety off his Thompson and emptied a clip at the oncoming vehicle.

"Gimme your weapon and load this one," Joe said, as he handed Little Joe his Thompson.

The German vehicle stopped and began firing back. Joe emptied another clip at them and sped after Kelly.

The fire in the canal still cast an eerie glow on the horizon to the north when Joe caught up to Kelly. The Halftrack was stopped about 200 feet from the Lagarde/Va Court Road. Fischer and Petuko, Thompsons at the ready, watched intently as the blackout lights of the Jeep approached. Joe stopped the Jeep behind the Track and walked to the driver's side. He let out a slight groan as he pulled himself up on the running board.

"What's the damage, Kelly?"

"Everybody here seems to be okay, how about you."

"I've felt better, but not since we landed at Omaha. Look, Kelly, Little Joe has picked up Oddball on the radio, but he hasn't heard us yet. These pack radios are only good for three miles in the best of conditions. We have to establish contact with them before we get to Avricourt."

"Right, Joe, I got no idea where they are. I will stop again at the Moussey/Remoncourt road and we should be in range by then. If not, we need to find a place to hide till tomorrow night. Or, do you have a different idea?"

"No, not now. Let's go when the coast is clear, I'm right behind ya'."

It was 0330 before Little Joe got through to Oddball.

"Big Joe, I got Oddball on the horn." Joe grabbed the mic from Little Joe and flashed his blackout lights. As Kelly came to a halt Joe said, "Oddball...where the hell are you?"

"We're in a forest about 3000 meters on a 292 back azimuth from Check Point One. Keep to the farm roads when you get close so you won't make tracks across the open fields."

"Roger, Oddball, we should be there right at dawn."

"Roger, Big Joe."

Big Joe pulled the Jeep in front of Kelly and led the way. They successfully crossed the Moussey/Remoncourt Road and made their way through the large forest to the west of Avricourt. They both crossed the railroad tracks to the southwest of town. By 0400 they linked up with Oddball.

"Kelly, see what equipment and ammo we've got left."

Kelly swung up on the back of the Track and started to figure out what was left. Joe checked the map with Oddball. Soon they were all gathered round Joe's Jeep.

"Okay Kelly, what's left?"

"Fischer's weapon is missing. We only have one bazooka with three rounds, one 30 cal machine gun and six, hundred round belts. Also, there are two M-37 Satchel charges, maybe 1000 rounds of .45 for the Thompsons and 15 magazines worth of loose rounds for the BAR. Willard has 12 full clips in his belt plus one in the weapon. Two boxes of grenades, one is opened with twelve missing, that's a total of 38 Grenades and 50 jerry cans of gas, that's…"

"250 gallons…what about a weapon for me," Fischer asked?

"I got a Thompson in my tank that you can have, along with about 350 rounds of ammo."

"Thanks, Oddball."

"No problem, Fischer, I've got a bigger gun up there."

"Sounds like a couple of good fire fights and we're done."

"Right, Petuko, our *only* hope is complete surprise. We've got nine miles to cover cross country to Niderhof, that's right at the base of the mountains. Then 20 miles by road through the mountains, we shouldn't have much trouble using the mountain roads. The Jerrys are moving a lot of stuff by rail at night. The troops in the rear are guarding the bridges that the Resistance is blowing to stop men and equipment reaching the front. If you see that cross with double cross bars the FFI has made its presence known. Keep an eye out, it usually is painted on the side of buildings with white paint."

"What time do we leave, Joe?"

"Kelly, let's make it 2100, things will have calmed down by then, and the Jerrys will have started to move behind their lines; three tracked vehicles and a Jeep won't be very noticeable in case we are spotted."

Kelly nodded.

"Two guys awake and on watch until we leave. Twenty-two of us and one Kraut Colonel, fourteen hours till we leave. Two and a half hours each should do it. Keep your eyes peeled and keep quiet. Oddball, you and your guys take the first five watches. Wake me and Kelly around 1430 and we will take it from there."

"Right, Big Joe, Moriarty, you and Rocky take the first watch, I'll watch the radio."

"Thanks, Oddball, thanks a lot for the first watch."

"Can it, Moriarty, everybody gets a turn."

"Crap!" Moriarty was chewing on his unlit cigar as he walked away towards the edge of the woods.

Big Joe was thinking about tomorrow morning and the end of the line, good or bad it would be over. He was rolling plans around in his head, as they all were. This was also the time to think about Corporal Job, Mitchell and Grace and mourn their passing. In the grand scheme of war these few people were the only ones who would notice they were gone. They all were, by now, on the rolls of the missing. Up the chain of command, they were just 25 MIA's and as you went further up the chain, all of us became acceptable losses or light casualties.

CHAPTER 7

Town of Schirmeck, France
0500 Hours 14 September, 1944

Sturmbahnfuehrer Zentgraf returned from his journey to search for gasoline. He woke the new second in command, Sturmhauptfuehrer Staerker. Zentgraf had taken over when Obersturmbahnfuehrer Vogel had failed to return. Because travel during the day was extremely dangerous, Zentgraf had left on the night of the eleventh and spent all day in Strasbourg. Even his threats as an SS Major didn't get him gasoline, simply because there was none to be had. The next night he went to Karlsruhe where his luck was much better. Zentgraf arranged for a fuel truck to arrive in Schirmeck on the night of the fourteenth or the morning of the fifteenth. Based on the promise of fuel, he gave Staerker orders to have the Tigers resume their routine of running their engines 15 minutes every four hours beginning at 0600. This practice had been temporarily extended to once a day due to the shortage of gasoline. This kept the engine's coolant circulating so the engines wouldn't overheat when started. *Everything was good; they would be in Switzerland by the night of the 16th was his thought as he went to get some breakfast.*

Big Joe, Kelly, Fischer and Gutowski had slipped into the sleeping town at 0445. Kelly had silently taken the guard out with his knife on the railroad bridge. They made their way in the inky darkness, up the *Grand Rue,* toward the church in the center of town. SS Colonel Vogel had told them what they needed to know about the layout of the town and the disposition of the troops that were guarding the gold. So far, he'd been correct. Big Joe told him that his uniform had been in Cowboy's Track, and was lying at the bottom of the Marne Canal. Vogel had responded that he didn't care; he knew he was now part of their operation.

The first light of dawn was still two hours away. Kelly could make out the vague outline of a tank near the church in the waning moonlight. All four men hugged the buildings as they made their way along the *Grand Rue* to the church. The heavy church door creaked as they carefully opened it. Their eyes, which had adjusted to the light from the sliver of a moon, detected the silhouette of a Tiger about 50 feet away. The imposing Panzer was parked in the center of the road effectively blocking the way. Big Joe noticed that the tank pointed towards the church, but the turret was leveled in the opposite direction. The radio operator, who was also the machine gunner, was obviously asleep, hopefully, along with the rest of the crew. The radio operator and the driver were the only ones in a position to spot their movements. Fischer stayed in the dark area next to the stairs while the others carefully walked up to the church steeple. The three would-be thieves climbed the ladder to the very top of the steeple, just under the cross. There were floor to ceiling louvered shutters in the cupola. This afforded a 360 degree view of the town, just like Colonel Vogel had outlined.

Kelly whispered, "I'll go and take out the highway bridge guard before Oddball comes through and hitch a ride on his tank. That way we'll be sure he makes it to the right position."

Big Joe said softly, "Okay, Kelly, I'll go back and get everyone else moving. Oddball said that the Tigers crank their engines every three or four hours for 15 minutes. We'll use that as our signal. We'll go one minute after the Tigers shut down their engines. You got that Gutowski?"

"Yeah, Joe, I'll pick off the guards that I can see. I think there is a machine gun on top of the big building where the gold is supposed to be."

"Send Fischer up and I will brief him before I go to the bridge," Kelly added.

Joe was down the ladder and gone by the time Gutowski got the sniper rifle unslung from his shoulder and set it down. He also laid his Thompson on the floor, along with the magazine carriers he had. He only had twenty rounds for the sniper rifle; it was a bolt action Springfield with a telescopic sight, not something you would use to stop an assault. By the time he got situated, Fischer had come up the ladder and was testing the walkie talkie.

"Little Joe, radio check, over."

"Loud and clear, has Big Joe left yet?"

"Yeah, about 5 minutes ago."

"Roger."

Big Joe made his way down the street. There was still no visible movement around the Panzer parked near the church. It was getting a little lighter as he crossed the railroad bridge because the moon came out from behind the clouds. Kelly, in the meantime, had made his way to the highway bridge near the approach. The SS guard was not alone, as he had hoped. There were two men on the bridge, one on each end. He hid in the bushes ten feet from the end of the bridge, between the abutment and the house that was right next to it on the street. *This is gonna be trickier than I thought.* Fischer watched intently as Sturmbahnfuehrer Zentgraf drove up and met Sturmhauptfuehrer Staerker out in the courtyard just below the church. Luckily, he could hear most of the conversation between the two Germans. He waited until Zentgraf went into the building next door to the church. Staerker went to each of the tanks and gave the sleepy crews their orders.

"Little Joe, Fischer over."

"Go ahead."

"Tell Big Joe they are going to crank the Panzers at zero six hundred."

"Wilco, anything else?"

"Yeah, the building catty-corner to the church looks like where the troops are billeted, just like Vogel said."

"Roger"

Little Joe gave Big Joe the information and went back to keep watch on Vogel.

"Okay, looks like they are gonna crank their engines at zero six hundred. We need to be at the jump off point before 0615. It's 0517 hours now so we only have fifty-eight minutes to get in position." Joe was checking his watch as he spoke.

Everyone understood. Jonesey and Penn mounted Oddball's tank before he pulled out slowly to the edge of the woods. Big Joe, Crapgame, Petuko and Babra got onto Whiskey's Sherman. Crapgame grudgingly hefted the .30 caliber before climbing aboard. Each one of the four had a 100 round belt of .30 caliber ammo draped around their necks. Cowboy handed Big Joe the bazooka to hold while he swung himself onto the tank. Willard handed Cowboy the bag with three rockets before he swung himself onto the tank. Oddball and Whiskey waited for Joe's signal. Big Joe moved to the assistant driver's hatch where Chuck's head was poking out.

"Gimme your earphones and mic."

"Sure, Joe."

"Fischer, has anything changed?"

"Negative, Joe. There is more activity down there, but nobody has come out of the building yet."

"Move 'em out, Oddball." Joe's voice was, as usual, steady as a rock even though it wasn't very loud.

The two Shermans reached the road intersection near the railroad bridge where Jonesey and Penn jumped off the tank and headed for the bridge with Big Joe, Babra, Petuko and Crapgame leading the way. It was 0530 when they all got across. Jonesey and Penn each carried a Thompson and two magazine carriers with five clips per carrier and one of the satchel charges. They knew they had about 45 minutes to cover the 500 meters to their objective, which was a three story building. They had to climb to the roof and then 100 feet over the rooftops of two buildings. Fortunately, there was only three feet between the two roof edges. Both the roof of the building that they were scaling and the roof of the billet building, which was an old French hotel, had very large overhangs. They might just make it.

* * *

Jonesey and Penn had no trouble. The *Grand Rue* did about a 25 degree right bend just before the church. Anyone on the east side of the street was not only in the shadows, but was also out of sight of the Panzer just past the church. They both stood at the wall of the three story building.

"Can you make it up that drain pipe, Jonesey?"

"I don't know, Penn, but it doesn't look like I've got much choice."

He set the Thompson against the building and took off the clip carriers and the satchel charge.

"Gimme that rope, Penn, and I'll give this a whirl."

Jonesey climbed up on Penn's shoulders using the pipe for balance and support. The drain pipe seemed to be sturdy enough and with his hands and feet he began to climb. The going was slow until he was about six feet from the top. He let go with one hand, grabbed the gutter and pulled himself up. He lay still on the roof for a minute before he crawled to a position six feet up the rake. Jonesey took the coil of rope from around his neck and let it down. Penn tied all the equipment to it, except his Thompson and clip pouches. Jonesey slowly pulled the equipment up to the roof. He lowered the rope once more and scooted further back from the edge. Jonesey anchored the rope by winding it around his body and holding it with both hands. Penn, using the rope, climbed onto the roof with the Thompson slung on his back. After Jonesey put his equipment back on, they crept along the top of the roof of the last building across the street from the church. Then they jumped the last three feet to the billets.

Jonesey found a line of roof access doors on the church side of the billet building. He carefully lifted the center trap door and could see the stairs below in the dim light. They both crept down the stairs. Penn stopped on the second floor, Jonesey went to the first floor and stopped short at the stair door. He carefully opened it and looked through a small crack. He spied what looked like a restaurant with two men sitting at tables. He quietly closed the door and laid the charge in a corner by the outside brick wall under the stairs. He crept up to the second story and waited by the stairs for his partner.

Penn had taken a few minutes to find a covered table in the hall that ran along the front of the building. He placed his charge under the table next to the outside brick wall and crept back towards the stairway. He passed the half opened doors of several rooms filled with sleeping German soldiers. Suddenly, a toilet flushed and a man opened the door midway down the hall to the stairs. Penn pulled his knife and waited for the SS soldier, who had gotten up to use the toilet, to go back down the hall to his room.

Each took up positions on the roof of the adjoining building and waited. They both had pulled the starting pins on British red, thirty minute, number 10 delay fuses at 0548 before they had entered the building. Each satchel charge had two of these pencil fuses, just in case one failed. The fuses had a plus or minus 2 minute delay per hour. Both men were glad to get rid of the extra 22 pounds of satchel charge. They crossed the roofs, climbed down the drain pipe and took up a position covering the front of the billets.

Big Joe, Babra, Petuko and Crapgame had about 600 feet to travel, mostly through backyards, gardens and woods after they split up with Jonesey and Penn. Finally, they stopped behind a large house catty-corner to the gold house in a clump of trees and bushes. Its ideal location commanded a clear view of the church, gold house and both the Panzers behind the church and the one on the *Grand Rue.* The going had been slow. Willard held the .30 caliber while Crapgame and Babra climbed over the first stone garden fence. Babra had grabbed the belts of ammo from Big Joe and Petuko before he went with Crapgame. Crapgame and Babra set up the .30 cal on the next fence and they had a good field of fire on the side door of the billets.

Babra pulled the tab on the belt of ammo until the first round in the belt stopped on the cocking handle. He pulled the handle back and eased it forward, chambering a round. They ducked behind the wall and waited. Big Joe went over the last fence and into the woods behind a long building on one side of the plaza. The northwest side was covered by a deep forest that rose up behind the town on the side of a large hill. The forest was close to a large house situated directly across the plaza from the church. It was a short sprint through an alley to the trees. Joe surveyed the Panzer to his left, behind the church, and the Panzer to his right, at the intersection behind the gold house. He could just see the muzzle brake on the 88 millimeter gun peeking out from behind the gold house.

Petuko set his BAR down near the shop at the end of the alley next to the billets and crouched by the corner. He watched the guard walking towards the shop in the alley. When the guard turned toward the town square Petuko stood up and quietly covered the four feet between him and the unsuspecting sentry. He grabbed the SS soldier's chin, covering the man's mouth, pulled his head back and with one fluid motion cut the guard's throat. He lowered his limp body to the ground and opened the door to the shop. Petuko dragged the body inside with one hand, holding the BAR in the other. He then opened the shutters and the window onto the alley. There was a field of fire covering the side entrance to the building. Joe could cover the back door and Petuko's position. The four positions had a field of fire on the entire plaza and the front, back and north side of the building.

* * *

The first light of dawn was showing as Gutowski spotted two sentries on the roof of the gold building and had each one of them in his sights. Fischer knew that if Oddball and Whiskey weren't successful at getting into position they would all be toast. As soon as the Panzers started their engines there would be no turning back. He could just make out some movement in the bushes across the plaza and he had watched Jonesey and Penn on the building across the street until they disappeared down the side of the three story building.

* * *

While the others were positioning themselves, Oddball and Whiskey had slowly and carefully driven towards the jump off point across the railroad tracks at the next road intersection. Fischer had spotted them about half way between the jump off point and the railroad bridge. He couldn't hear their engines, but just to be safe, he told them to stay put. The town was just starting to wake up, no reason to hurry the process. Oddball stopped, as did Whiskey.

* * *

At 0600, when SS Sturmhauptfuehrer Staerker walked across the street in front of the church and blew his whistle, he was in sight of the Panzer in the square and the one in front of the church. Within fifteen seconds, both Mark VI engines sprang to life. The third Panzer cranked up 20 seconds later after the first two engines had started. The roar was deafening to anyone in the square. Fischer gave Oddball the go ahead and they both took off.

Whiskey stopped momentarily to let Cowboy and Willard off with their bazooka and the three round canvas carrier. Whiskey did a 90 degree turn, rolled over the stone garden wall and over the next three walls until he came to the building behind the church. It was a garage and the double doors opened into the back of the building. Wally, the loader, and Murph, the assistant loader, got down and opened the doors. They pushed a small Renault sedan out of the garage and guided Whiskey's tank into it. Wally opened the front door a crack and looked out onto the square. He shook his head and got up on the vehicle.

"Whiskey, you got a perfect angle, but the damn Tiger is facing us. We can't penetrate the front slope."

"Let me look." He scrambled off the turret and

looked out the door. "Damn it, just our luck. We'll go for the turret and hope we can scramble their brains. We'll get two shots, and then we have to move if he's still alive. Let's get to it boys."

Murph stayed by the door while Wally and Whiskey got back in position. Wally loaded an AP round in the breech and they waited.

Oddball's tank raced along the *Avenue de la Gare* that paralleled the railroad tracks towards his hide. He turned at *Place de la Gare* where the Avenue de la Gare made a 90 degree right turn towards the center of town. Moriarty poured the coals to it on the straight stretch. Just before the tank turned the corner, the two SS men on the highway bridge turned to look towards the approaching vehicle. Kelly jumped the man closest to him and with one fluid motion covered his mouth, jerked his head back and slit his throat. The noise of the approaching Sherman held the other guard's attention at the other end of the bridge. Kelly ran full tilt and hit him with a flying tackle as he raised his weapon to engage the Sherman which had just appeared around the corner. The rifle went flying and Kelly jumped to his feet, and lunging forward he drove the knife into the back of the man's neck. Oddball stopped and Turk got down and helped Kelly throw the two bodies into the rushing stream. They both got onto the tank as it lurched forward, Moriarty was in a hurry.

Moriarty raced up the *Avenue de la Gare* and slowed

down only to turn the corner a block before reaching the *Grand Rue*. He stopped, let Kelly off, and continued up the curving street. Moriarty slowed to a crawl as the Grand Rue came into view. He stopped about 50 feet from the intersection. Oddball dismounted and walked to the corner. He walked back to the tank and lowered himself into the hatch.

"What's it looking like, Chief?"

"It's a Mark VI and we got it by the ass." Turk rotated the turret so it was 90 degrees to the right and lowered the gun slightly.

"Load an AP round, we only get two shots, so we gotta make 'em count. Look sharp everyone, this is it."

Kelly ran the 100 feet to the last storefront on the north side of the street and broke the glass in the door. He went inside and from the door and the display window he had an unobstructed view of the front of the building that billeted the SS Troops. He, Penn and Jonesey had the front door in what would become a deadly crossfire.

Suddenly, he heard someone open the door behind the counter. The shopkeeper stood in the doorway with a shocked look on his face. He assumed that they were Americans and scowled. Kelly put his finger to his lips and held up his Thompson. The man retreated upstairs. Hopefully all was ready. In less than five minutes Staerker blew the whistle and held his closed fist high in the air. Everyone was in position, for good or bad. In one minute the show would begin!

CHAPTER 8

Schirmeck, France
0616 Hours
14 SEPTEMBER 1944

"Go Moriarty Go!"

And go he did. The Sherman tank leaped forward and covered the 50 feet to the intersection in record time. Turk made final adjustments with the elevation and traversing wheels as the vehicle lurched forward. Moriarty slammed on the brakes. Turk pressed the foot firing switch as Oddball opened up with his 50 cal. on the German tank Commander who was visible in the main hatch. The German fell back into the tank with half his upper body gone. The M62A1 Armor Piercing shell cut through the engine compartment like a hot knife through butter and exploded inside the tank. Debris spewed out of the open main hatch. The ruptured gas lines poured fuel over what was left of the engine.

"Into the square, Moriarty. Turk, get the turret forward there is another Tiger in the square." Oddball bent down in the open turret as Jesse loaded another AP round. Moriarty skillfully drove the 33 ton Sherman into the narrow street next to the gold storage building as Turk brought the turret to the forward position. The stricken Tiger was rolling black smoke now and the first of the rounds inside cooked off. The explosion lifted the turret almost off the mainframe and the fire was temporarily blown out. Oddball raised himself out of the turret for a look around.

"Hug the building, Moriarty! Turk, fire when you've got a shot! We got this one by the ass too."

"I'm on it, Chief." Turk answered automatically as he has done dozens of times before.

By the time the Tiger that was behind the church in the courtyard started its engine, Murph had thrown the front door open and scrambled aboard Whiskey's tank. The German tank Commander saw the door open out of the corner of his eye. He whirled around and barked orders to the crew. The turret was starting around towards the garage. The German assistant driver opened up with his MG 34 machine gun spraying the wall of the building. The rounds went through the plaster walls and ricocheted off Whiskey's tank.

Wally had zeroed in on the back of the German turret and he fired. The round exploded when it hit the turret, only partially penetrating the steel. Wally loaded another round and zeroed in on the right drive wheel of the Panzer whose main gun now pointed toward them. Murph scrambled toward the turret.

"Get the front drive wheel, Barney, back us outta here…Now!"

Barney floored the gas pedal and the tank lurched backwards as Wally fired. The Tiger fired to the right of the open door as his right track separated and fell off the drive wheel. Barney had his foot to the floor and was half way out of the garage when the round impacted the right side of the front slope. It didn't penetrate, but ricocheted and exploded in front of the turret. Chuck, the assistant driver and Murph, the assistant gunner, were killed instantly. Everyone else in the tank was wounded. Barney was trapped, he couldn't get his hatch open because it was under the main gun. The German tank Commander and his loader jumped out of their stricken tank and ran towards Whiskey's crippled Sherman. Both men had a maschinenpistole 40. The Commander was about ten feet ahead of the loader when a burst from Fischer's Thompson rained on him from the church tower. The loader whirled to fire and was cut down with the second half of the clip.

On the other side of the church, the German gunner was loading another 88mm round when a 75mm round from Oddball's tank cut through the engine and exploded in the crew compartment. It was a 75 yard shot, but the armor piercing round did its job. The tank started rolling black smoke and three minutes later the first of many rounds cooked off.

When the fireworks started, Willard and Cowboy had slipped around the corner across from Whiskey's hide. Cowboy kneeled down with the bazooka on his right shoulder. Willard slipped a rocket in the back of the tube, wound the ignition wire around the pole and tapped him on the helmet. After the German Tank Commander and loader were cut down by Fischer's Thompson, the German gunner stood up in the Commander's hatch to see what was going on. The whoosh of the rocket from Cowboy's bazooka caused him to whirl in that direction as the rocket impacted between the turret and the main body of the tank. He quickly withdrew into the tank and closed the hatch.

"Feind um drei!" He shouted and the assistant gunner immediately rotated the turret towards the three o'clock position.

The 57 ton monster was a sitting duck without the right hand track. The assistant gunner saw Cowboy get up and run behind the building just before he fired. The 88 mm armor piercing round went right through the corner of the building just behind Cowboy and exploded when it hit the wall 20 feet beyond. The explosion blew a huge hole in the front wall of the clothing store and debris showered both of them while they were on the run. They ran about a hundred feet before a third round went through the building and finished the clothing store.

Gutowski took out one of the German machine gunners on the roof of the gold house while he was frantically looking for a target for his MG42 machine gun. He quickly worked the bolt on the Springfield sniper rifle and got the other machine gunner before he figured out where the shot had come from. As several Germans came out of the front door of the billet building, Penn could hear Petuko's BAR hammering them, as well as Kelly's Thompson. Two men came out the side door near the tank and they were immediately mowed down by Crapgame and Babra manning the .30 cal. Gutowski took out the SS Master Sergeant Staerker as he tried to make it into the billets. Suddenly, there was a terrific explosion on the second story of the billets and two men were blown out of the windows above. Less than 15 seconds later the satchel charge under the stairwell of the bottom story blew out all the windows and doors and brought the second story floor down on the survivors. The explosion caused most of the wall of the building near the tank to collapse.

The dust and smoke obscured Kelly and Petuko's line of fire as they ran out of the store across the street. They hugged the wall of the gold house and stayed hidden by the dust. The German assistant driver was firing in the direction of Crapgame and Babra. But both of them had abandoned the .30 cal when the German gunner had stopped to put another belt in the MG34. The smoke and dust of the explosion obscured the German gunner's view for 30 seconds, that's all the pair needed to get to the corner of the gold building. The gunner was disciplined enough to not fire unless he had a target.

"Oddball, it looks like Whiskey's hit." Fischer picked up the walkie talkie when the building blew.

"On my way, Moriarty, get over to Whiskey past that Tiger. They're hit."

Moriarty drove from behind the building gaining speed as he crossed the street in front of the down, but not out, Tiger. The gunner in the Tiger was looking for a target when Oddball's tank came out from behind the gold building. He didn't have time for a carefully aimed shot, so he took a chance and hit the firing switch. The 88 roared, the round glanced off the very rear of Oddball's turret, and impacted the house across the street from the gold house. It destroyed the kitchen. Oddball breathed a sigh of relief when he heard and felt the round glance off the spare track that was partially wrapped around the turret from the three to nine o'clock position. The force of the round cut the spare track in half. Moriarty maneuvered behind the church before the loader could get another round in the breech. Cowboy and Willard had found a narrow passage between two buildings and moved carefully towards the street where the wounded Tiger sat.

The dust was just settling from the explosions when they came out onto the street. Cowboy knelt down and Willard loaded the last rocket round into the five foot long tube. He secured the trigger wire and stepped back into the passageway. Cowboy took his time because it was his last round and he had this one by the ass. Luckily, the turret was pointed the other way. Cowboy was taking no chances as he stood up and moved three steps closer. He figured he was within 30 meters of the Tiger and that he would put the round right between the two large tubes on the rear which were part of the deep water fording equipment. Cowboy pulled the trigger. Whoosh! The round made a loud clunk when it sliced through the engine compartment and, almost instantly, a muted explosion came from inside the tank. The hatch blew open and within 30 seconds the tank began rolling black smoke as the gasoline ignited. Two minutes later the first rounds heated up and exploded.

Oddball arrived at the garage and they all ran inside. He had Rocky, the assistant driver, call Fischer and tell him they needed help. The tank was still smoldering, but luckily it hadn't exploded. Whiskey and Wally were pinned in the vehicle by the debris from the wreckage of the garage's second floor. Both men were bleeding from their ears and from many cuts due to shrapnel and flying roof joists. Both of them were semi-conscious. Oddball's crew began clearing the debris away from the turret while Turk was trying to rotate the turret to the right to set Barney free. There was blood all over Barney when they pulled him, semi-conscious, from the driver's seat. Sadly, most of the blood belonged to Chuck and Murph, who had absorbed most of the blast. Ten minutes later all three were laid out in the square and were receiving Jesse's capable first aid.

After Cowboy and Willard took out the last Tiger, Big Joe, Crapgame, and Babra went around the corner to the front door of the gold building.

"Fischer, any movement in this building?" Big Joe was holding the walkie talkie to his ear.

"Gutowski popped two guys on the roof when the fireworks started, but no movement now."

"Yeah, one of 'em is lying on the other side of the building. Do you see Cowboy and Willard over by the Tiger?"

"Yeah, they're staying clear until the ammo is finished cookin' off."

"What about Petuko and Kelly?"

"They're going through what's left of the building that blew. Jonesey and Penn are down by the wreckage, too."

"Barbara, get over there and get 'em here pronto!"

"The name's Babra, Joe."

"Yeah, Yeah, just go!" Joe put the walkie talkie to his ear again and pressed the transmit button. "Oddball, what's happening?"

"Whiskey's tank was hit. We got them all out. Murph

and Chuck bought it. Wally is hurt, but not real bad. I think Whiskey and Barney are gonna' be okay. Ya need help?"

"Not yet, but get that thing out in the square in case we have to use it."

"What about that last Tiger?"

"Cowboy and Willard got it."

"With a bazooka?"

"Yeah, with a bazooka. Fischer, you and Gutowski keep the civilians in their houses and make sure your eyes are peeled for stragglers, especially snipers."

"Will do, Joe."

"Ya think there's anybody inside?"

"Now what do you think, Hustler, is there anybody inside? You want to walk through that door and find out?"

"Okay, okay what'll we do now?"

"Wait for Kelly and Petuko, you go around back and make sure no one squeezes through the bars on the windows."

"Right." Joe rolled his eyes and shook his head as Crapgame trotted off towards the back of the building.

Kelly and Petuko came running up. "What's up Joe?"

"I figure there's got to be at least two to five guys in there. We gotta smoke 'em out without getting' killed."

Joe reached over and tried the door, making sure he was protected by the stone wall. The door splintered as a burst of machine pistol fire raked the door. Joe pulled his arm back.

"Does that answer everybody's questions?"

Kelly and Petuko nodded.

"Petuko, get Cowboy and Willard over here. Kelly, let's break all the windows."

When Petuko got back, he had Cowboy and Willard with him, but he also had found Jonesey and Penn.

"Cowboy, you got any rounds left for the bazooka?"

"No, Joe, all gone."

"Finish breaking the windows all around, don't get yourselves shot, okay?"

They shot out all the windows, except for the two front windows. The people inside obliged by shooting them out from the inside when Kelly knelt down and raised his helmet up. The soldiers inside shot at anything that moved.

"We go when I shoot out the lock on the front door. Everyone choose a window and pull the pins on two grenades each," Joe ordered.

The moment Joe's Thompson began to chatter they let the spoons on each grenade fly, counted to five and threw them though the broken windows. Before the grenades went off, there were shouts from inside the massive old building. Joe counted to three, kicked the door open, and jumped inside shooting as he went. Kelly did the same on the side door, spraying the room with his Thompson. Both men pushed the magazine release. The clips dropped to the floor and in one motion they both jammed clips into their weapons and released the bolts.

Petuko was right behind Kelly holding his fire looking for a target. A grenade came bouncing end over end down the stairs.

Kelly yelled, "Grenade!"

Big Joe was still at the door, but jumped quickly outside. Kelly and Petuko fell to the floor. It was two seconds before the grenade went off sending furniture and wall debris flying, along with body parts from the dead men who were on the floor by the stairs. Immediately, Petuko emptied a magazine into the floor above the stairs. They all heard a yelp and the thudding of a body rolling down the staircase.

Kelly, Big Joe and Petuko spent the next five minutes checking the bodies of the fallen SS soldiers. Then all three went up the stairs and cautiously inspected each room and closet. They even went into the attic. They were satisfied that the six bodies were the last Germans in the building. Everyone but Fischer and Gutowski were gathered around the stacked boxes in the middle of the room.

"I'll say one thing for the Krauts, they're neat," Cowboy observed.

In the middle of the floor were 350 wooden boxes, each marked with a German eagle, a swastika in its talons and the double lightning flashes of the SS. They were arranged in stacks, five boxes high, seven rows wide and ten deep. Kelly pried the top off one of the boxes. There they were, shiny gold bars *without* the

German eagle and SS runes. Each bar was 400 troy ounces, 27 and a half pounds of .999 percent gold! They were neatly packed four bars to a box. Everyone in the room was transfixed on the amazing sight before them.

Then Big Joe broke the silence. "Let's get 'em loaded and get the hell outta here. Move it!"

Suddenly, they were shocked out of their stupor. Crapgame went across the square to the German trucks that were parked in a neat row. He started the first truck and drove across the square to the front door of the gold house.

"Listen up, it looks like we got six trucks. Those boxes weigh about a hundred pounds each..."

"Every bit of it!" Willard interjected while picking up a box and stacking it on one of the two hand carts they had found. They had actually found four, but two were victims of debris from the burning tanks in the square.

"Thanks for that. These trucks have a payload of about 7000 pounds, so it looks like we load 70 boxes per truck. And the sixth truck is for us. Fischer, call Little Joe and have him drive the Track over here."

"Roger, Joe."

"Jonesey, get those other trucks over here. We all gotta have German uniforms. So pick out the ones with the least amount of blood and holes and pull 'em off the bodies."

They had just finished loading the second truck and

were backing the third one up to the door when Little Joe drove up.

"How's the leg?"

"Maybe a little worse, is that the gold?"

"It sure is, did you get everything out of the Jeep?"

"Just like you said, Joe. What's my job?"

"If you can walk, find some uniforms that aren't full of holes or soaked with blood. We each need one."

"That's disgusting, Joe, can't someone else do it?"

"Sure, you can take his place loadin' the gold."

"I'll get the uniforms."

"Let's start filling' these trucks with gas from the Track, Whiskey's tank and my Jeep."

"How much in each truck, Joe?"

"Fill 'em up, Jonesey, if you can and if there's extra, put it in the Kraut Jeep. Then, if there is any leftover, put it in the empty jerry cans. The trucks with the gold get the gas first. Put the empty cans in the trucks too, just in case we need 'em."

Jonesey just nodded. It was already half past seven in the morning, the sun was up and the three Panzers were still burning fueled by the gasoline, ammunition and bodies. The air smelled foul.

It had taken them about an hour to load four trucks. Everybody was concerned about being attacked by the Air Force, so they all started working like men possessed. Fischer arrived about fifteen minutes later with the German Jeep and the extra hands were sorely needed for the loading process. None of them had realized how long it would take to load 350 boxes, each weighing just over 100 pounds. That's over 35,000 pounds. Not one single person in the group had any inkling of how big a heist this was; nor just what repercussions it might have in the near or distant future. As with most robberies all the planning went into the committing of the crime and little went into what to do afterwards. Most robberies fall apart during or shortly after the getaway.

CHAPTER 9

Schirmeck, France
0745 Hours 14 September 1944

"Big Joe, this is Little Joe."

Joe lifted the walkie talkie to his ear and answered, "yeah, what's goin' on?"

"We got company, three trucks coming down the mountain from the north. Looks like they got troops on board!"

"How far before the edge of town?"

"About three miles, they are coming down the mountain to the south about two miles from my location."

"Are you still on the hill to the west of the south road?"

"Yeah, Joe, I'm about a mile from where the black smoke is coming' from."

"Is there enough cover up there to hide all these trucks?"

"Yeah, I'll go down to the crossroads and direct 'em in."

"Good!"

"Oddball, take the Sherman down to the railroad tracks and head south on the main road. Go past where you see Little Joe and stop those German trucks, take out as many as you can. Kelly, you take all our trucks down to the railroad tracks, Little Joe will take it from there. Leave one guy at the road junction behind Oddball. I'll catch up when we finish loading the last truck."

"Get a move on Joe 'cause we got a long way t'go," Kelly said, jumping on the lead truck.

Joe hurried to the gold house and began hoisting boxes onto the back of the truck. Penn was in the back moving them to the front of the vehicle. Willard and Petuko were loading the last five boxes on the hand cart.

Cowboy met Willard coming out of the building. "How many more, Willard?"

"That's it."

Cowboy dropped the hand cart and ran towards the empty truck. "Follow Kelly, Cowboy!"

"That's what I was a thinkin'."

Willard, Joe and Petuko loaded the last five boxes.

"Drive this thing, Willard and follow Cowboy. Petuko, you get in the back and cover him."

Joe and Penn turned and ran toward the truck park. Joe threw his Thompson between the front seats and he and Penn jumped into the German Jeep. Joe cranked the engine, ground it into first gear and raced off after the last truck.

Moriarty pushed the Sherman for all it was worth down the highway.

There were six German Borgward b3000 trucks behind him, five loaded with gold, and the sixth with desperate men. They had no plans from here on.

Oddball told Jesse to load an HE round, they wouldn't need armor piercing for trucks.

"Check your weapons everybody, Moriarty, can't you get any more out of this thing." Oddball was surprisingly positive except when it came to Moriarty.

"It ain't gonna go any faster, Oddball, even if you push!"

A minute later Oddball saw Little Joe's Jeep at an intersection off to the right on the main road.

"There's Little Joe, Oddball, what do I do?"

"Go 100 feet past the intersection on the road coming off the mountain and stop. Turk, you get ready to blow anything away that comes around the bend up ahead. Jesse, you get ready with another HE and maybe we can get all three."

Kelly jumped out of the lead truck and began giving orders.

"Little Joe, lead these trucks up the main road a ways and keep your eyes peeled. Fischer, Jonesey, Gutowski come with me, Oddball's gonna need some help."

They all ran down the road towards Oddball's tank.

Before they were half way there a truck, loaded with troops, came around the slight bend in the road. Turk fired as the driver tried to stop. The High Explosive round impacted on the radiator grille and blew the truck and the people in it to pieces. The truck behind him had just started around the curve, it swerved off the side of the road, and landed in the ditch. When Turk fired the next HE round most of the men in the back had been thrown out or jumped. The shot was in the right door, the explosion sent pieces of the truck and rained flaming gasoline down on the men who had jumped or been thrown free. Kelly's group ran past the tank towards the burning trucks. Moriarty began to move forward at about the same speed as Kelly's men. Kelly slowed down as they reached the burning vehicles. He signaled Gutowski and Jonesey to the other side of the road. There was no one left alive in the first two trucks. From the looks of the bodies, they were all SS troopers. Kelly and Fischer made their way around the fiery wrecks in the ditch. Gutowski and Jonesey crawled in the ditch on the other side of the road and Gutowski laid his Thompson over the top and fired half a clip. The Germans in the third truck had dismounted about 50 meters from the curve. They had taken up positions in the ditches on both sides of the road. They returned fire not knowing exactly what they were firing at.

Joe drove like a man possessed down the first alley he could find that ran parallel to the main road. Shortly, he could hear the firing off to their left and could see the intersection about 200 meters ahead. He drove toward it. A young SS trooper stepped out from behind a building on the street ahead and hesitated, recognizing the vehicle as an SS Jeep. It was too late for him by the time he realized that the men in it were not SS. A short burst from Penn's Thompson ended the war for him.

Joe stopped at the intersection at the edge of town.

The walkie talkie crackled, "Oddball, come up here and hit these fuckers with HE," Kelly urged.

"Willco baby."

Moriarty stopped short of the burning wreckage and Turk depressed the 75 mm gun while Jesse loaded a HE round into the breech.

"Ready, Turk."

Big Joe keyed the mic switch on his walkie talkie and said, "Hold your fire."

"Hold your fire, Turk." Oddball looked surprisingly calm for the moment.

"Put one close enough to jar their back teeth, but try not to kill 'em."

"Okay, Big Joe." Oddball leaned down to Turk and smiled as he said, "Turk, give 'em a reason to surrender."

A large grin spread across Turk's face as he moved the main gun to the right and slightly up.

"Fire when ready," said Oddball, sporting the same sized grin.

The 75mm HE round streaked through the air and

landed about 30 feet to the right of the ditch. It made a screeching sound as it passed over the heads of the men in the ditch.

"Hände hoch, steh auf und geh diesen weg!" Within 30 seconds, 20 very young SS troopers stood up, put their hands up and walked towards Fischer, as ordered.

When they got within 15 feet of Kelly's position, Fischer shouted, "Bleib stehen und steh da." All 20 men stopped and stood quietly.

"How many are left in the ditch?" questioned Kelly.

"Wie viele sind noch im Graben?"

"Vier," replied an older member of the surrendered group.

"Are the four wounded?"

"Sind sie verwundet?"

"Nein."

"Oddball put a round in the ditch."

"Turk, put a round in the ditch on the left."

"Willco Oddball."

Turk swung the turret left and lowered the barrel. He looked at Jesse who gave him the thumbs up and Turk pressed the foot trigger. The explosion sent two bodies eight feet in the air, arms and legs were flailing, and they hit the road like rag dolls. Almost immediately, two men on the right side of the road stood with their hands up and walked to join the men who had already surrendered.

Big Joe had watched the scene from the Kuebelwagen

with Penn. He keyed the walkie talkie mic. "Oddball, Little Joe, lead the trucks to the nearest hide for the day and get everyone undercover. Kelly, you and Fisher get in the last truck and tell Cowboy to hold it there. Fischer, get those guys' uniforms and throw them in the back of the truck, then follow Little Joe. Our Flyboys are gonna come lookin' in about an hour or two and a truck convoy will be too much for them to pass up. I'll catch up, I need to go to the other side of town and pick up the Kraut Colonel.

* * *

At 0947 two P-47 Thunderbolts flew over the hillside where the band of miscreants had parked and camouflaged the vehicles for the day. Kelly smiled as the P-47's threaded around the low hanging clouds that had moved in during the night. Their search pattern was catch as catch can because their attention was divided between looking for the enemy and dodging the fast moving clouds. Kelly and Big Joe were encouraged that after flying over their area, the fighters turned and went back north after only ten minutes. Maybe tomorrow they could travel a little longer in daylight without worrying about being caught in the open in what was now an SS convoy: six trucks with a Sherman Tank leading the way and a German Kuebelwagen bringing up the rear. Hopefully, this is the southern edge of their search area.

* * *

All the men, to include the wounded, had changed clothes. After dark, Kelly and Fischer had gone into the little town of Fouday at the bottom of the hill to get a doctor for Whiskey, Barney and Wally. The doctor showed up and was quite happy and sympathetic as he treated the three wounded Americans. He was obviously not a Nazi fan. Fischer did all the talking and was very generous with the doctor, giving him two hundred French Francs for his trouble. The doctor thanked him very much for the Francs knowing full well that the Allies were just weeks away from driving the Third Reich back into Germany. Then, Reich Marks would be only good for starting fires or lighting cigarettes.

Oddball, Big Joe, Crapgame, Fischer, Kelly and Colonel Vogel poured over the map for about 20 minutes before deciding which route to take. If they could make it to Saint Nabord by tomorrow morning, then they could lay up outside Lure the next night. The plan seemed good. This was the first chance they had had to figure out what was next. As close as they could figure, they had enough gasoline to go another 200 miles if they left the Sherman behind and transferred the gas into the trucks. The initial plan of splitting up the gold and going their separate ways wasn't going to work, they had to do something different and they had to do it soon.

CHAPTER 10

The convoy had stopped at 0600 and the vehicles were camouflaged as artfully as before. They had all finished breakfast and were gathered together for a meeting. This would be their first discussion since the attack on Schirmeck two days ago. They hadn't addressed the elephant in the room, what about the gold? When were they going to split it up and get on with their lives?

Big Joe started off the meeting. "We got some thinking to do and some plans to make."

"What about the split, Joe? Little Joe piped up while most of the others mumbled agreement.

"Here's the problem and it's one that no one, especially me, ever thought of. There are 21 of us counting the Kraut Colonel..."

"Who included him?" Little Joe interrupted.

Most of the men voiced their concerns with a "Yeah, who the hell included him?"

"Hear me out, you, Little Joe, zip it," slightly raising his voice. Little Joe nodded.

"As I was saying, there are 21 of us and 350 boxes of gold. That works out to 66 bars each, or about eighteen hundred pounds. We are in France, in case no one noticed, how are you gonna smuggle eighteen hundred pounds of gold back home...Aboard a troop ship?" You could see the light go on in the other faces.

"That's almost a ton," Babra whispered and no one said a word.

"Does each one of us want to find a place to bury it and come back after the war is over?" The silence was deafening.

"We need a place to keep it and a plan on how to get it to the states."

Most of the heads in the group bobbed up and down in agreement.

It was Crapgame's turn, "I think it should be put in a bank where it will be waiting for us later. We have to figure out how we are going to get back to the states without Uncle Sam figuring out what happened. We lost five good soldiers and it took a lot of hard work for what's in those trucks and we want to enjoy it." Again, heads nodded.

Big Joe took over. "This evening we cross the border into Switzerland as an SS truck convoy. Fischer, you put on the Colonel's uniform. Colonel, you put on the German Major's clothes and, remember, you're part of this. If you do anything to give it away, you will be dead in a heartbeat, versteh?"

"Only too well, Sergeant, I have left my former life as an SS soldier behind. We, who have brains, know that the war is lost. I must make the best of what is left of my life. I am a practical man, I don't believe my future lies in the ruins of Hitler's Third Reich. It lies in the back of these trucks."

"So, everybody else, get those SS uniforms on and put Whiskey, Barney and Wally in uniforms that have blood and holes in 'em, it'll look good to the border guards. Siphon the gas that's left in the Sherman and put it in the trucks. We all go in the six trucks and the Kraut Jeep."

"What happens when we get to Switzerland, boss?" asked Petuko.

"We find a bank that wants German gold." Crapgame's slightly sarcastic reply said it all.

* * *

Kelly stopped the Kuebelwagen at the red and white

striped pole barrier. They had all been briefed by the Colonel about how the border crossing was constructed. There was a three meter high fence with three strands of barbed wire on the curved portion at the top of each pole. The curve was towards France, meaning it was meant to keep people from leaving France. There was a concrete pillbox about 15 feet from the pavement on the right side of the road and a tower about 30 feet from the edge of the left side of the road. Both were manned with MG-42 machine guns, nicknamed "Buzz Saws" because of their phenomenal capability of firing 25 rounds per second. Their only drawback was the barrels overheated after only about 250 rounds. A good machine gun crew could change barrels in less than 20 seconds. That was when an enemy would time their attack against the gunner. The addition of a second gun in the tower made it impossible to take advantage of that drawback; the guns covered each other during barrel changes.

It was about 100 meters between the fence and the border posts, marking the actual border. This 100 meter wide strip of land was a mine field full of "Bouncing Bettys." The hapless person that stepped on one of those saw the mine leap to crotch level and explode; there was no way to get away from it. That, coupled with at least ten soldiers at the crossing, made it foolhardy to try to fight your way through it. The only smart tactic would be to do what Fischer and the Colonel were about to do. They got out of the back seat of the Kuebelwagen and handed the Bills of Lading and passes to the Hauptscharfuehrer, who apparently was in charge. Fischer knew that this was the US equivalent of a Master Sergeant so he would know what he was doing. If there was an officer at this crossing, he didn't show himself.

He read the papers carefully and asked why the three Panzers and the other three trucks weren't there. If they were coming later, if so, the Panzers would have to wait here; the Swiss would never allow them into their country.

"Verdammet Amerikanische Luftwaffe!"

"Schade." The look on his face made it apparent that "too bad" was just something he said to appear concerned, he really didn't care.

Fischer was able to pass off Whiskey, Barney and Wally as three survivors of the three trucks and three Panzers they had lost. Petuko and his BAR were also in the back covered with a blanket. The Colonel had suggested that Petuko play dead because he looked Spanish; it was easier that way rather than trying to explain how a Spaniard had made it into Das Reich, 1st SS Panzer Division. All three wounded men played the *1000 yard stare* role very well, the sergeant didn't ask any questions about them. All three walked the length of the column back to the lead vehicle. The Master Sergeant handed the Bills of Lading and passes back to Fischer, who passed them to the Colonel. He then clicked his heels and threw his right arm up in a Nazi salute simultaneously with a "Heil Hitler." The Colonel immediately returned the salute crisply while Fischer's reaction was a little slow. The sergeant lowered his arm and said, "Gute Reise, Herr Obersturmbannführer."

Fisher nodded and replied, "Danke Hauptscharfuehrer."

While opening the truck door for Fischer, the Colonel observed, "He was not pleased with your return of his salute. The SS is very conscientious about their salute and Heil Hitler; hopefully, he doesn't take it to heart."

"Hopefully." Fischer's face was dead pan and he watched the Master Sergeant instruct his men to raise the barrier and motion them through.

"Slowly, Kelly, we're not out of the woods yet."

Kelly nodded and drove forward towards the Swiss Border. The last two trucks were still in France when the Kuebelwagen stopped at the red and white striped barrier. Fischer started to dismount, but the Swiss Border Guard motioned for him to stay in the vehicle. He studied the Bills of Lading and their passes to leave France and to enter Switzerland and said, "ein moment." He turned and went into the small building to the right of the road.

The guard spoke into a phone and said something, then listened attentively. A minute later he hung up the phone and returned to the Kuebelwagen. "Alles in ordnung," and he turned immediately to signal the man standing by the barrier.

"What'd he say?" Kelly was getting a little antsy.

"Everything's okay," replied the Colonel, smiling to no one in particular.

The last two trucks drove past the barrier and everyone breathed a sigh of relief. The mountains of Switzerland rose in the distance with snow already forming white caps on their peaks.

All of them were dressed in German SS uniforms and carrying German weapons. They rode in German trucks with over 19 tons of German Gold with no clear idea of what lay ahead. They all felt safer than they had felt since they left the states over 9 months ago.

PART III

CHAPTER 9

AFTER I MET WITH UNCLE Jerry, there was one high point in the months that followed. The electronic precautions that I had taken paid off. Three days after I disabled the four trackers in my car, a three man team showed up at 0316 on the morning of May 15th. They did very impressive work, quickly, quietly and without wasted motion. All three men were gone by 0329, having planted four more trackers. The trio wore balaclavas, but one of them had rolled up his sleeve while he was working in the trunk. He exposed a tattoo on his right forearm that was kind of strange and rather humorous: Snoopy in his World War One fighter pilot's garb. This was the same trio that had gone over the house on Oleander Drive in Panama City Beach on the night of November 25th last year. They had planted cameras and listening devices. I decided not to bother the bugs in the room because they would just be back to plant more. Also, I had rigged their burst transmitter that I had found in the car to a homemade battery box and moved it to a more convenient location in the trunk in an old cigar box. It occupies the cigar box with the other three trackers and a battery operated LED light to keep the solar powered trackers charged. When I want to go somewhere that I don't want them to know about, I simply leave the box in the condo, strategically placed in sight of one of my "hidden" cameras. Who would notice or care about an old cigar box?

As you can see, I gave up on the "frozen north" of Panama City Beach when I came back from my Dallas trip and moved south, like any bird with a brain would. Also, Rod feels better about the 6K a month rent instead of 40K. I believe one should live life to the fullest, especially if it is on someone else's dime.

To get down to business, I have read and reread the "Warriors" manuscript and perused the timeline for Kelly. I arrived at a conclusion. Namely, the heist in France is most likely a true story and not the story put out by the folks that want you to believe it was a joint crooked US Military and German Civilian enterprise after the war. After researching the names that I have, I have come up with a clue that may lead to the identities of Oddball and Crapgame. I went through everything that Rod got from his father's house with no luck, even wading through it several times. I received the military records from Ms. Jenkins about PAM and from what I could tell, he did in fact, assume someone else's identity to return to the States after the war. I knew what happened with PAM, but not the whole story as it pertains to this case. What I need now is the Rosetta Stone: something that will give me a bridge between what I've got and what I need. Unlike the Rosetta Stone, my source code remains hidden.

Over the last two months, the few leads that I had dug up died a slow death. Now, I'm off to interview my last lead. The elation I felt when I read "The Warriors" manuscript has pretty much evaporated in the last several weeks. It was like being all dressed up with no place to go.

It was late afternoon when I arrived at the front door of Steven Gregory Jr. in Sebastian Florida, just up the road from Vero Beach. I wasn't very hopeful because this had been too easy. He had answered his phone, something the vast majority of people in this country don't do anymore. We had a friendly chat and he said he would gladly talk to me about his father. The house was very nice, as was the upper middle class neighborhood. I rang the bell and in less than a minute a tall, slim man in his mid-sixties answered the door.

"Mr. Wallach, I presume?"

"Indeed, and you, I take it, are Mr. Gregory?"

"You are correct, please come in. Can I get you something to drink, it is almost 5 o'clock?"

"Whatever you're having, if that's okay."

"I'm having a rum and Coke."

"Even better, I love a good Cuba Libre, do you have lime juice and a slice of lime?"

"Of course, it wouldn't be a Cuba Libre without the lime, most people don't know what a Cuba Libre is, so I just say rum and Coke."

"Mr. Gregory…"

"Steve please, my father was Mr. Gregory and he's been gone almost a year now."

"Steve then, I'm Nick, what can you tell me about your father's time in the Army."

"Not a lot, Dad didn't talk about his time in the service."

"Did he go to reunions or have a group of old veterans he hung with?"

"He used to go hunting every year at his cabin in North Carolina. He was usually gone for two weeks and if I recall correctly, he never brought back any trophies."

"Do you have any names of the people that he might have gone hunting with?"

"I have his old address book."

"Could I see it?"

"Certainly." Steve got up and walked to a cabinet in the living room and retrieved a black, leather bound book and handed it to me.

"Most of the people in that book are business associates or contacts. The back two pages are his close friends, I think."

I spent about five minutes skimming through the book, no name leaped out at me. Then I turned to the first of the three pages in the back and again, no joy. The next page however was pay dirt. The name reached out and bit me, WJR!

IT JUST CAME TO ME LIKE A THUNDERBOLT AND I REMEMBERED MY LIST!

WJR-33***382-Private First Class-Item Company, 137th Inf-MIA 12 Sep 44 Retd 1 Feb 45 HOR Intercourse, PA-Born 15 Jun 24-Died Tinicum Township, Bucks County, PA 18 Jun 2009

I didn't need the list that I had made up to recognize the names, each and every one was burned into my brain. I interviewed JR's daughter, Betty Johnson, near Longwood Gardens last September. She told me her father went to a reunion every five years in different cities, but now I find out that he also knew SAG!

Further down the page two more names leaped out at me JCK and JJK.

*JCK-38***895-Private First Class-Anti-Tank
Company Special Troops 134th Inf- MIA 12 Sep 44
Retd 1 Feb 45 HOR Happy, TX- Born 2 Nov 22-
Died Midland, TX 17 Aug 2004*

*JJK-33***983-Private-Battery B 161st FAB
35th ID-MIA 12 Sep 44 Retd 20 Feb 45 HOR
Pittsburgh, PA-Born 12 Dec 24-Memory Care,
Groton CT*

"You know, Nick, I had forgotten this, but he used to get together with some old Army buddies about every five years. Back in 2000 he had told me that they all had decided to stop getting together because it was getting too hard to travel. Most of the group were gone or in poor health. I think 2000 was the last time they got together."

Now for the 64 thousand dollar question. "Do you remember where the reunion was?"

"Somewhere in California, but I don't remember the name of the town."

"Carmel?"

"That's it! Carmel by the Sea, I remember because Clint Eastwood was the mayor there once."

I spent the next twenty minutes chatting with Steve and copying down the addresses of each one of the old man's friends from the last two pages. I finished my drink before asking my last question.

"I know this is kinda personal and feel free not to answer, did your father leave much of any estate when he passed?"

"Yeah, he did, he left it in trust for my two sisters and me. It seems like he got really good with real estate, along with fast food joints. Dad's hunting lodge, where they met, was a five bedroom, five bath house. He called it a cabin and it's on 250 acres of land near Franklin, North Carolina, if that tells you anything. He had several opportunities to sell it for big bucks, but he would never consider it."

"What would you say his estate was worth?"

"I don't really know because it is all in a trust and it pays each of us about two hundred and fifty thousand dollars a year. The trust takes care of all the rental properties and businesses and it spits out checks to use every year like clockwork."

"Sounds nice."

"It is."

"Here's my card, if you think of anything else, I would really appreciate a ring."

"Of course, nice meeting you and talking about Dad, he was quite a character from where I stood."

"You know, Steve, from what I have gathered, he was just that, quite a character."

I high fived myself as I got in the car. The investigation was alive again and I had more work to do. When I got back to the condo, I left my personal laptop in my briefcase and activated the spare computer that I always left on the desk. It indicated that I had an email. I didn't open it until I had typed some "notes" into the computer and then I opened it. *1636 Intrusion video captured.* I double-clicked the mp4 attachment in the email and watched the eight minute video of a guy hacking into my computer and downloading several files that were labeled *Kelly Investigation.* He was so intent on not missing a golden opportunity and so confident that he took off his balaclava. I printed a screenshot of his face and his Snoopy tattoo and put it in a paper file that I kept in the computer bag. I went to dinner.

Later, when I came back from dinner I took the cigar box back to the car and I checked the spy program, and in the words of Oddball, "I had him by the ass." The culprit had downloaded a file that I had "hidden"on my hard drive labeled "Notes on the Warrior manuscript." It contained a hidden spyware program that gave me a backdoor into his computer. I spent the rest of the evening searching his computer for any clue and came up with next to nothing. All I had to show for my efforts was their computer password , their secure Wi-Fi information with its password, my "notes," and an IP address. I would have been very disappointed if they had downloaded my information into one of their own personal computers; that would have given away the amateurish nature of their skills. They were pros, they had my planted information, but I knew where the computer was and I was going to take a little trip to visit them.

I verified the names and addresses copied from Steve's father's address book and they checked out. I needed to make a trip and I didn't want company, so I had to visit my "tails" base of operations. I called Scotty on one of my burner phones and told him what I needed. He had always loved a little excitement, so he agreed to my proposal, and we set it up for tomorrow. I bought a ticket on-line via Elite Airlines from Vero Beach to Newark, NJ for tomorrow and packed my bags. A mere five minutes after I booked the flight my "tails" booked two seats to Newark on the same flight. I packed my bags and went to bed.

CHAPTER 10

MY PHONE ALARM WENT OFF at 0330, I shaved and showered. At 0400 hours, leaving the cigar box behind, I drove to the physical address that I had gotten from their IP address. It was an older duplex near I-95 in Ft. Pierce. It was an easy set-up and pretty straight forward. I placed my "spy box" on the ground near the internet service cable and got back in the Benz. Using my phone, I connected with their Wi-Fi in my planted "spy box." Using the Trojan Horse provided password, I broke into their secure Wi-Fi and then set up an SSID. That made my entry into their network seem like just another password protected Wi-Fi network. And, Bob's your Uncle, I was in! I could see everything they did on any computer connected to their Wi-Fi. I drove back to the condo and crawled back into bed at 0630 and didn't stir until almost noon. I had to get some beauty sleep because when you look like me, you need all the beauty sleep you can get. At 2:44 PM that afternoon I arrived at Vero Beach Airport, parked the Benz in the free long term parking lot and walked to the terminal. I spotted the tattooed computer hacker in the passenger waiting area, but he didn't seem like he was looking at me. I ducked into CJ Cannon's restaurant and found an empty table.

20 minutes later, and after I had finished a cup of really good coffee, Scotty walked in. I greeted him and we both slipped out the front door. After getting into the Sun Aviation's courtesy car, we arrived at Sun Aviation three minutes later. I paid for Scotty's fuel at the counter while he went outside to do a walk around on his King Air 200. I climbed into the right seat, just like old times in Afghanistan. We went through the startup procedure and were soon ready to taxi.

"Vero Clearance Delivery, November two two three Tango Oscar, IFR to Shreveport, Louisiana."

"Roger, November two two three Tango Oscar, you are cleared direct to Treasure VORTAC, Victor one five nine to Cross City VOR, direct PICIS Waypoint, Shreveport Regional Airport, climb and maintain Flight Level two five zero, contact Departure on one two three point six two five, Squawk four two two one."

"November two two three Tango Oscar, cleared direct to Treasure VORTAC, Victor one five nine to Cross City VOR, direct PICIS Waypoint, Shreveport Regional Airport, climb and maintain Flight Level two five zero, contact Departure one two three point six two five, Squawk four two two one."

"Read back correct, contact ground on one two seven point four five, good day."

"Ground one two seven point four five, thank you and good day."

"Ground, November two two three Tango Oscar, ready to taxi."

"Roger, three Tango Oscar, taxi runway Three Zero Left, hold short landing traffic."

"Tango Oscar taxi runway Three Zero Left, hold short landing traffic."

Scotty gently pushed the throttles forward and taxied to the hold short line on runway Three Zero Left.

"Nice with the radios, you haven't forgotten, in how many years?"

"Thirteen and thanks." I tuned up Treasure VORTAC and folded the chart so I could keep track.

"Three Tango Oscar Taxi position and hold, landing traffic Three Zero Right."

"Roger, taxi position and hold landing traffic."

"Roger."

"If my tail is waiting for me, we'll find out at the end of the line. I'm not gonna worry about it till we land."

Scotty just grinned.

"Three Tango Oscar cleared for takeoff."
"Three Tango Oscar rolling."

We refueled at Signature Aviation in Shreveport where we bedded the aircraft down for the night. The cute blonde at the desk gave us the keys to a crew courtesy car and we made our way to the Airport Hampton Inn, just across the street. We enjoyed dinner at Crawdaddy's Kitchen, a hearty recommendation by the desk clerk at the Hampton.

We took off from Shreveport at 0930 with a refuel. We made an aircraft and crew stop at Cutter Aviation at Albuquerque International Sunport. *Sunport, instead of airport ... seems a bit presumptuous to me, oh well, who am I to question?* At least the Frontier restaurant was really down to earth with very good Mexican food and homemade tortillas. They didn't put on any airs. We arrived at Montgomery-Gibbs Exec Airport in San Diego at 3:45 and were driving out the front gate by 4:30 in a rented Toyota from Gibbs Flying Service, heading to El Cajon Boulevard, a 20 minute drive to the south.

Scotty used his credit card for the rooms at the Lafayette Hotel and Club on El Cajon Boulevard. My expense account from Rod had ponied up two grand for this trip with the understanding that Scotty would use his credit card for expenses. I was certain that whoever was following me had alerts on my cards and I didn't want them to know where I was and what I was doing. So far, so good; no one was waiting for us in San Diego. My phone was still back in Vero, can't be too careful. We had left Albuquerque on a VFR flight plan to Las Vegas. I had changed it enroute with Flight Service to land at Havasu City airport in AZ. We refueled at Havasu City and filed another VFR flight plan to LAX. When we called LAX approach, we switched our destination to San Diego. I knew that whoever was following us would have a very difficult time with us on a Visual Flight Plan instead of an Instrument Flight Plan.

Scotty spent the next two days by the pool and in the club. I phoned FRM on the afternoon that we got in and invited him to the club. He declined, but said I could meet at his favorite restaurant, La Fachada in Barrio Logan.

When I got to the restaurant I looked for the oldest guy in the outdoor dining area. There was an older guy sitting by the back wall eating.

He seemed to be totally engrossed in his dinner until I said, "Mr. Montoya, I hope?"

"Si, Senor Wallach, sit down." He motioned to the chair across the table from where he was sitting.

"Are you hungry?"

I hadn't been when I walked into the place. It was basically a food truck alongside a covered outdoor dining area next to a blue concrete block building. There was a charcoal grill in the middle of the courtyard sizzling with a platter of grilling peppers and onions. The aroma was all it took to get my taste buds demanding satisfaction.

"Now I am, what's good here?"

"Everything."

"What are you having?"

"Al Pastor Huaraches and Horchata."

"What's Horchata?"

"A rice drink flavored with cinnamon, sugar and vanilla, a lot better than a Coke or Pepsi."

"I'll try to remember Al Pastor Hua…"

"Just tell 'em to give you what I'm having, easier that way."

I went to the window and said, "may I have the same thing that Senor Montoya is having?"

"Si Senor, good choice."

I walked back to the table where Montoya was sitting, still enjoying his meal. I knew he was born December 31, 1925, so he just turned 92 years old. To his credit, he looked maybe early 80's. I sat down and asked, "do you know why I'm here?"

He nodded his head.

"What can you tell me?" At this point I was expecting a wall or curtain to come down, but the opposite was true.

He smiled, wiped his mouth and asked, "you want to know about Kelly's Heroes?"

To use the old, "you could have knocked me over with

a feather," would be lined through by the editor, but that's how I felt.

"Are you willing to talk about it?"

"Only if you buy my dinner." He smiled the smile of someone who has a secret that he knows you want to know.

"Done!" We both laughed. "I have twelve names, could you verify they are the individuals you pulled the heist with?"

"Let's back up a little, *Muchacho*. It wasn't a heist, it was a battle with a group of SS *Pendejos* and we kicked their asses. Now what came afterwards was just taking the *spoils of war*."

"Understood, you were doing your job and took the *spoils of war* into protective custody."

"We're gonna get along real fine, Nick."

"How did you know my name?"

"Word gets around."

"Can you give me any more names than the ones I have?"

"Let me see the list."

I gave him a copy of my list of names and he nodded, wiped his hands on a napkin and started writing on the paper. I tried very hard to not peek at what he was writing down. I didn't see much until he handed it back to me and I was speechless. He had written down the names they used in the manuscript next to each of the names on my list. This was it! "The Warriors" was real, and if that wasn't enough he had written down two more names at the bottom of the page.

PAM-Kelly, DHP-Jonesey, JJK- Gutowski, JAT- Penn, WJR- Fischer, FRM-Petuko and the two names at the bottom were DRS-Oddball and LBN-Turk.

I now had the Rosetta Stone that I needed to get the information on Oddball's group. I only needed the last three members of Oddball's crew: Moriarty, Rocky and Jesse. Also, Whiskey's crew: Wally and Barney. He told me that he thought that Turk had passed away, but he hadn't heard if Oddball was still around. The last he knew was that he was up in LA, but that was three or four years ago.

"What did you do after the war? I still don't know what happened to the gold?"

"That's not for me to tell, but I did pretty well. I got into the import business back in '51 and was really successful. I started importing Volkswagens, Toyotas, Hondas and Datsuns before they set up plants here in the States. I still own seven companies in Mexico that supply the VW Plant in Puebla, Mexico. VW makes 2250 cars a day in Puebla, mostly for export. There is no shortage of work for my companies."

"How about reunions?"

"We had mini reunions every other year with different groups, but we all got together every five years, until 2000. We had started to feel our age and some of the guys' health took a nosedive, so we stopped the big get-togethers. I did make each one because I'm still in good health."

"Can you tell me about Cowboy, Willard, Babra, Jonesey, Gutowski, and Penn? How did things turn out for them?"

"Sure I guess that's okay, let's see, ah, Cowboy and Willard, they both ended up owning a slew of big farms and each had a huge ranch. Willard had his place in Arkansas near Little Rock, I think, and Cowboy had his place in Texas, west of Ft. Worth. Both were into cattle and farms in Kansas, Nebraska and Oklahoma that raised cattle feed. They figured that if they raised their own feed, it would increase their profits. Then there was the oil. Neither one of them had to farm or ranch with the oil wells and leases they owned, but they enjoyed it."

This is beginning to sound familiar. "Did they also start to prosper around 1950?"

A sly grin and narrowed eyes replaced the look of nostalgia. "I see you aren't just another pretty face."

"Thanks, I know there's nothing pretty about my face."

He had to laugh at that one and continued, "Babra and Jonesey went into the construction business together and did a lot of building in Jersey, New York and Pennsylvania. I think they even had something to do with building the World Trade Center and I know they built several places in Atlantic City. Babra lived in Jersey and Jonesey, Long Island, but I think they're both gone. Babra about a year after 9-11 and Jonesey in '06 or '07, I'm not sure which."

"2002 for Babra and 2007 for Jonesey." Checking my notes.

"Penn and I knew each other quite well. He moved here after the war and got involved in the movie business. He ended up becoming a producer and owned two production companies. He also owned a really big ranch in Montana. We used to go there during the summer just to get away. Penn was involved with me in a couple of companies in Mexico and since we both love tequila, we bought a couple of farms that raise Agave. We also bought interests in a couple of local distilleries, all in all quite profitable. Penn died in '05 and I was really sorry to see him go, we had some really good times."

"And Gutowski?"

"That's a sad one- he had two kids, a couple of years apart, Steve and Thomas, I think. He also was quite successful up in Connecticut as a defense contractor. He was big in the stock market up until the late seventies. His oldest son was killed in Vietnam, I think that was Thomas. Then, his youngest, Steve, went to flight school and onto Vietnam as a helicopter pilot. He waived the sole surviving son restriction before he left. He went missing on a night mission with the 101st during Lam Son 719 in 1971. They declared him Killed in Action, Body Not Recovered in '78. Gutowski spent the next 30 years in Thailand, Cambodia and Vietnam looking for him. He got Alzheimer's around '05 and he's just hanging on in a rest home in Connecticut. I saw him five years ago, but he didn't remember me, and thankfully he has all but forgotten what happened to his kids. Very sad, he was *really* sharp. His company specialized in stuff for the Special Operations people. Little Joe said Gutowski got involved with the Corsican Mafia when the CIA told him to "piss up a rope" when he went looking for his son. According to Little Joe, Gutowski made a lot of enemies in the Agency. But because of his companies' influence and the big hitters on his Board of Directors, they couldn't do anything about it. Little Joe seemed to think that Alzheimer's is a dodge to keep the Corsicans and CIA off his back. I don't know. And you know about Fisher,

Little Joe and Kelly. Ask Oddball about Big Joe and the tank guys 'cause they got really close."

I watched him finish his Huaraches and down the last of his Horchata. He wiped his mouth and said, "All that, even the reunions, were a long time ago. I was young when we did what we did and it has been good for me every minute since. I was lucky, Corporal Job, Mitchell, Grace, Murph and Chuck weren't. We all made sure their families have been very and I mean *very* well taken care of, it's the least we could do."

I noticed his eyes water ever so little as he spoke of the men that didn't make it. He looked away, but when he looked me in the eye again, he smiled and said, "Nothing, before or since, has been so exciting. War is the worst thing that mankind has come up with, but if you survive, you know more about yourself than anyone who hasn't been there. The fears that govern most people are not even an annoyance. An emergency is when someone is dying, everything else is routine."

"Good way of looking at things. Have you thought of anything else that you can tell me?"

He smiled, shook his head and got up to leave. He left a hundred dollar tip on the table and sauntered outside. He didn't look as spry as I imagine he did in 1944, but he moved with a certain rhythm and maybe what one would call a spring in his step. He exuded an air of confidence that only a person totally at ease with himself and his life could have. I hope that I am half the man at 80 that he is at 92.

CHAPTER 11

I CALLED THE NUMBER THAT Petuko had given me for Oddball and heard a very soft spoken female voice, one of those voices that you can't put an age or a picture to. She told me where to be and when, in a friendly, but business-like tone. I complied and here I was ringing the doorbell.

The door opened and the voice was the same as the one on the phone. She was a fiftyish woman with medium length blond hair. She was thin with an athlete's physique. Pretty, not drop dead beautiful, but with a smile and eyes that gave her incredible sex appeal. She looked like a woman that would tear your clothes off with her teeth and roll you in the hay until you couldn't stand up. Even with all that racing through my mind I simply said, "Nick Wallach, Miss." I hoped it was Miss and not Oddball's wife.

"Linda...Linda Phillips and Miss is correct."

Hooray, I calmed my libido knowing that this woman could twist just about any man around her little finger and I really had work to do.

"Follow me, Doc is on the patio."

She opened the sliding doors and there he was, Oddball, in all his shining glory: long hair perfectly styled in what I would call the "1970 Clint Eastwood look," think *Dirty Harry* or *Play Misty* for me. He had a dark, modified Fu Manchu moustache that ended in a goatee. The moustache was dark brown until it reached the goatee and then the hair turned snow white. He was casually dressed in chinos, golf shirt and sandals. I knew he had to be in his early to mid-nineties, but he didn't look a day over 75. I'm sure that he had had a bit of "nip and tuck." This was not the Oddball I had expected at all.

"I see you met Linda, without her, I would be lost."

"Mr. San..."

"Call me D.R. or Doc as most do," he interrupted.

"Doc, I feel certain you know why I'm here. I would like your perspective on what happened in 1944."

"You have the manuscript which I co-wrote with Crapgame-back in the '60's when I was trying to get the story out without anybody knowing who the real people were."

"Can you give me some insight into the two tank crews: Whiskey's and yours?"

"Linda, would you give me that sheet with the guys' names on it?"

"Certainly, Doc," she said, handing him a single sheet of paper which he glanced at and gave to me. I read it with a certain amount of sadness.

LBN-Turk-Clifton New Jersey-Died July 17, 2009-Lung Cancer

GCK-Wally-French Lick, Indiana-Died August 2, 2006-Complications from COPD

KKH-Rocky-Buena Vista, VA-Died January 15, 1989-Car accident

JJS-Jesse-Dallas, TX-Died March 15, 1999-Heart attack

MAK-Whiskey-San Antonio, TX Died August 30, 1988-Motorcycle accident

RBM-Barney-NYC, New York-Died September 11, 2001-Tower 1

RAW-Moriarty-Jupiter, Florida Hospice Care-Kidney failure complications from diabetes, not a transplant candidate

LMT-Crapgame-Weggis, Switzerland, **Parkstrasse

RTM-Big Joe-Manhattan NYC, New York
disappeared the evening of December 31, 1995
Declared dead January 15, 2003 by the State of
New York.

"That is pretty sad, Doc. Except for Moriarty and Crapgame, they're all gone."

"It happens at this age, but they all lived full lives and left estates worth between 15 and 25 mil to their heirs. I'm really sad about my mechanical genius, Moriarty. He built a string of auto garages all over the world. He ran a school to teach mechanics that was affiliated with schools in Florida, he really was interested in that. He just reads and watches TV now, he has good days and bad, but he got tired of the dialysis. He decided to stop it this month and I'm very sad to see him go, but he's had enough."

"What about Big Joe, what's the story there?"

"He was a person of interest in a homicide back in '92. The cops were giving him a hard time."

"Enlighten me, please."

"All I know is his wife was kidnapped and turned up dead after he paid the ransom. The cops thought he was behind it and kept at him for a couple of years, but they never could get any evidence. You know, the old "gut feeling." The detective in charge had a closed mind and wouldn't look anywhere else for answers. He swore to all of us that he had nothing to do with it. If I remember correctly, he hired several private detectives, but they came up empty. Finally, in '95 he disappeared and within two years there were a bunch of gangland style murders in and around the city. Mostly low level types, but they all had been in considerable pain before they expired. We were all pretty sure Joe was just grabbing mob guys and, shall we say, "questioning" them. The victims had lots of burns, missing fingers or toes and broken bones before they died. When Joe got a hair up his ass, he was capable of anything. We all have our suspicions, but no one really knows. Up until his wife was murdered, Joe was doing really well. He had a bunch of apartment houses all over the city and upstate, Troy, I think. He was really big in the fast food business and had car washes all over the eastern seaboard. He had two sons, one was a National Guard soldier and died in the Gulf War. The kid, Jack, I think was his name, left a wife and three grown kids. They got Joe's estate because his oldest son, I think his name was Bill, dropped out of sight right after Joe did. That's about all I know except the murders stopped about the time Joe and his son disappeared. I think they "got" him and his body is in the mucky Meadowlands in Jersey and maybe the kid too, who knows?"

"Quite a story, it reads like a crime novel."

"Joe really loved his wife, he met her in '49 or '50 and they had a really good life. Their mansion was on an estate near Montauk, quite a place. I was there several times. They lived the life out there until she got kidnapped. He probably got fed up with the cops and their constant innuendos and hassles.

The cop that headed up the investigation died of a heart attack about six months after Joe went missing. I figure Joe found out who was behind the death of his wife and he went after them, that's why the killings stopped in New York. I think that if you want to find Joe, you need to look someplace where a bunch of bad guys are dying that have a connection with the New York Mob. You probably will find Joe and his son there if they aren't in the Meadowlands. That's just my thoughts."

"It doesn't sound like Joe has any intentions of dying of old age in a hospice or in his own bed."

"I think you are right on the money."

I asked Oddball about his life and he wasn't very forthcoming. He described himself as a fixer. I gathered from his conversation that he facilitated the removal of problems and the smoothing of pathways to success. I thought it was more like a go-between. If you wanted someone gone, or a sticky problem solved, Oddball was your man. More power to him, I guess he enjoyed giving people "an edge", just like he did in 1944. I had a feeling that Oddball was heavily involved with what Big Joe and his son were up to, but that would require a lot more investigation.

I left his place and reluctantly said goodbye to Linda Phillips and her form fitting black pants, loose white blouse with the top two buttons undone. Also, those three inch spiked heels reminded me of what my late wife called "catch me, fuck me shoes." I still didn't know if there was anything going on with her and Oddball, but something told me I would spend some time in the future finding out.

If you're paying attention to the story, my next stop is painfully obvious. I made my way back to the San Diego airport and found Scotty at the hotel. I told him that I had paid for the rest of the week for him to enjoy himself and gave him another two grand to have a good time. At the airport ticket counter, I dropped five grand of Rod's money on a business class ticket to Zurich, leaving at 6:10 PM. A glance at the clock on the wall behind the ticket counter said I had just enough time to get through security and to the gate.

CHAPTER 12

TUESDAY MAY 29, 2018
Hotel Beau-Rivage Weggis
Weggis, Switzerland

"THIS IS THE MOST CHARMING place I have ever lived in." *These* are the words on a plaque under an old oak tree where Mark Twain used to sit when he and his family lived in Weggis in 1897. He actually said, as reported in a biography by Albert Bigelow Paine, "This is the charmingest place we have ever lived in for repose and restfulness, superb scenery whose beauty undergoes a perpetual change from one miracle to another, yet never runs short of fresh surprises and new inventions. We shall always come here for the summers if we can."

It is very inspiring to walk along the same path and probably view the same old hotels and restaurants that Mr. Clemens so fondly spoke of 121 years ago. With your back to the lake, look at the majestic Mt. Rigi that rises suddenly in front of you. Turn around and you are on the shore of the awe inspiring Lake Lucerne. Across the lake rising higher than any other mountain in the area is Mt. Pilatus. The Rhododendrons blast forth in every color from a very deep dark red, lightening to a pleasing pink and then white. There was a horn blast from an arriving lake ferry that ran to all the little towns that have sprung up along the tranquil shore over the last 900 years. War has never touched this place. The closest battle was the Battle of Sempach that occurred in 1384 between forces of the Swiss Confederacy and the Hapsburg Austro-Hungarian Empire. Sempach is 26.5 miles north of this paradise by road, 12 miles as the crow flies.

Lake Lucerne's peaceful lapping waters, the aromas of excellent German cuisine, huge swathes of color from flowers, and assorted swaying palm trees makes this spot a paradise. That's right, palm trees, cabbage palms to be exact, in this mild climate. It is the Swiss counterpart to the US's South Carolina.

From my hotel I walked Goddardstrasse for about two blocks and turned onto Seestrasse which followed the lake shore towards the Mark Twain monument. I walked past the Central Hotel and Restaurant where the road turned into a pedestrian/roadway and the speed limit dropped to 10 km per hour, a little over 6 miles per hour. It's probably easier to walk and it is only one lane wide. Past the boat docks to the stairs that go up the hill to Parkstrasse, sits Crapgame's house.

Normally I would call, but I don't have the luxury of a phone number, so it has to be a cold call. I rang the doorbell and two minutes later a woman in her mid to late 60's answered the door.

"Ja, kann ich Ihnen helfen?"

"Bitte, mein Deutsch ist nicht so gut."

Replying in a slight Bavarian accent she asked, "do you speak English?"

"Yes, I am looking for Herr Tygart."

"Please come in and your German is quite good, unless 'my German is not so good' is the only phrase you know." She said with a sly smile.

I had to laugh. "Nein, danke für das Kompliment."

"I suspected there was more, what business do you have with Mr. Tygart?"

"I'd like some information about his experiences during World War Two."

"I'm sorry, sir, but that Mr. Tygart passed away four years ago, I thought you meant his son."

"Oh, I wasn't aware."

This was a wrinkle I hadn't thought about seriously, although it was quite stupid for me not to. I'm tracking incidents that occurred 74 years ago when the people involved were young men. I have tracked down almost the entire group, 90% of them are gone. I hoped that my dilemma didn't show too badly. I was wrong there too.

"You look a bit perplexed sir, possibly my husband, Larry Tygart Junior, could help you. Could I get you a cup of coffee; you look like you could use it."

"Yes, thank you, Mrs. Tygart, you are very kind."

She turned and left the room saying on her way out, "my husband is on the phone now, but I will let him know you are here."

A few minutes later she returned. "The coffee is brewing; it will be a few minutes before it's finished. My husband indicated that he will be available soon, possibly you would like to have your coffee by the pool?"

"A pool…that sounds very nice." I was shocked again, maybe one in a hundred families in Europe has a pool."

She led me through the house which quietly spoke the language of serious money. The furnishings were contemporary and I guessed that half of the paintings on the walls were originals. The house itself was what I would call a step down house. It marched down the hill using a series of three and four steps down to the next level as we went down the hill. The outdoor pool was another anomaly because the vast majority of pools in Europe were located indoors: a nod to the extreme winters. But then again, Weggis had palm trees. I had seen several family pictures on my way through the house, so I knew what to expect when Larry Tygart arrived.

I was absorbed in the view of Lake Lucerne from the poolside. Mount Pilatus was very imposing, but the real beauty was in the flowers that dominated the entire view. Their spring colors raged and spilled over the vast landscape.

I could see why Mark Twain was so taken with the area, I doubted that it had changed significantly since he took it all in as he sat under that oak tree at the end of the lake side walk.

Larry's wife came in ahead of him with a coffee service on a silver tray and she promptly excused herself and left.

I stood up and turned around to meet a man that was a clone of his father. I even detected a slight Brooklyn accent. He was about five foot seven, approximately 150 pounds and looked to be in better shape than I had imagined his father had been when he embarked on the mission in '44 as a young man. He was bald and he shaved the vestiges of hair around the side of his head, like Yul Brenner or Dwayne Johnson. He was not relaxed, nor was he tense, at ease, but wary.

"I have been expecting you."

"Really?" I said rather naively.

"Yes, we have kept close watch on your progress. You have taken a little longer than we anticipated. But, you took the winter off in South Florida, I suppose to gather your thoughts."

"You are very well informed sir, I am allergic to winter. May I ask how you know so much about my movements?"

"We have been tracking you since you sent out those letters back in August of last year. We were informed immediately of each one and I've gotta say that you did very well, 38 of the letters were received by people associated with our little enterprise." He poured us both coffee and indicated the sugar bowl and creamer on the tray.

I picked up the cup and said, "I like it black, thank you. May I ask some questions, Mr. Tygart?"

"Larry, please, and fire away." He is his father's son, that phrase wasn't taught in a Swiss classroom.

"I think you are the last piece to a very complicated puzzle. I have the story up to what happened until your father and "Kelly's Heroes" crossed the border into Switzerland. Nobody has been forthcoming after that part. I understand why that is, the operation was illegal and all of them could have been charged with robbery and desertion at the very least."

"I'm afraid your thinking hits a snag there. The Allies confiscated boat loads of Nazi gold and everyone involved, except my Dad, returned to the states at the end of the war. Some with names they hadn't been born with, but they did return to the 35th Infantry Division in one capacity or another."

"Why just some of them, couldn't they all return under their own identities?"

"No, they were all MIA's, but they couldn't all be accounted for in the same manner, it would look too suspicious. Half of the 35th guys volunteered to take the names and records of soldiers who were Killed in Action or Missing in Action. That, of course, meant they couldn't go back home to parents, sweethearts or wives as a different person. The ones who were estranged from their families, or had no families, volunteered to become different individuals. Those soldiers were given temporary records, just enough to get them a discharge when they got back to the States. The other half went back as themselves."

"How did they do that without being caught? Someone, along the way, was bound to figure out that at least *one* of them wasn't who he said he was."

"Nick, may I call you Nick?"

"Of course, I'm calling you, Larry."

"Naturally, where was I...? Oh yeah, each one of the ships coming back to the US had between 2000 and 8000 people on board. Each person had to be on a roster and accounted for. The units reported to their higher ups and the ships recorded each soldier as they boarded. Big Joe's recon unit was half filled with new replacements and they were only able to get six of the original guys back into his unit. They were listed as having been absorbed by another unit when they had become separated from Big Joe's recon platoon in the heat of battle or, slightly wounded and detained at an aid station. The other six had to go another way and that was what they came up with. Four of the six reunited with their families later on, claiming they had amnesia from battle fatigue, I believe it's PTSD now. That was after 1956 when the war and what you did in it wasn't so important. A person did not need an honorable discharge to get a job."

"So, what about Oddball's unit?"

"Same thing, the eight survivors went back as what remained of the two missing in action crews. Before you ask, my father, "Crapgame", never went back to the States. He was and is still listed as MIA. He was a Swiss citizen, naturalized in 1955 with a Swiss passport and full citizenship. He was also a citizen of Paraguay from 1958 and he traveled to

South America on a fairly regular basis until 2000, when his health deteriorated. At that time I took over his job and have been carrying on in his absence."

"I would guess that this entire operation has to remain secret from the IRS. Correct me if I'm wrong: by funneling the possibly undeclared money to the families, the IRS boys would have a field day raping each and every person; and the estates left by the soldiers that pulled off the heist."

"I will correct you if you don't mind. The IRS was short circuited by my father's genius. I know that sounds like bragging, but it's true. My dad and Josef Vogel, the SS Colonel, who came into Switzerland with them, stayed behind when the others departed to rejoin the American Army. They deposited the gold in a bank in Bern. At the same time, they converted seven bars of gold into cash and gave each soldier 5,000 dollars. Each soldier was very happy with the immediate result of his labor. My dad and Josef were left with 1393 gold bars from the boxes that they had opened. Those 1393 bars stayed in the bank in Bern."

"So, each guy had 5,000 dollars in his pocket when returning to the states, plus all his back pay from Uncle Sam. Remember at the time a new car, if you could get one, was about 1000 dollars and a two bedroom house was about 3800 dollars. Each man would be able to go back, get a job or go to college on the GI bill. He could afford to live quite well on what the government allotted and his five thousand dollar bonus."

"What happened in 1949?"

"Well, Josef and Dad had incorporated a bank in Meiringen which is near Bern. They used the gold as collateral for bank loans when they started the bank near that little town. By 1950 they had done so well with financing companies involved in the rebuilding of Germany that they had a very long line of credit. They made loans to all the ex-soldiers who had participated in the heist. They were no-interest loans with extremely liberal repayment terms: *Pay back when you can.* Everyone took loans: anywhere from 100 thousand to two million and started businesses. By 1957 all the loans had been repaid, and any time they needed more money, it was transferred the same day. During that time the bank prospered enormously. Both Josef and Dad were millionaires several times over, in addition to their gold reserves. Presently, there is only one individual who borrowed money and has no intention of paying it back. It's still a loan, but we know he will not be sending any back."

"Who is it and why won't he send it back?"

"Big Joe and his son are in South and Central America hunting cartel members until they are all dead, or both of them are. They killed Joe's wife and they'll pay and pay dearly."

"Is that the only person that is in danger legally?"

"Yes, from a financial point of view."

"Do you have any idea of their whereabouts?"

"We only know the locations where we send them money as they request it. They notify us by code, for example, *Wish Little Jimmy a happy 20th.* That means send 20 thousand dollars to the drop, code named Jimmy. We know where the drop code named Jimmy is, but not when they will pick it up."

"What prompted your father to remain in Switzerland?"

"If the truth is known, I think it was initially the gold. He was worried that it would be discovered by the authorities and confiscated. Also, he had developed a real bond with all the individuals involved in the operation. He knew that they couldn't smuggle the gold back into the states without eventually being caught. Remember, it was illegal in the '40's to possess gold in the United States. Colonel Vogel knew how the Nazi organization in South America was going to utilize the gold they had robbed from European Treasuries and the Jews that they had executed. If you didn't know: we are Jewish. He ran what he called a "long con" in South America where he bilked the Nazi organization in Uruguay, Paraguay and Colombia out of millions in a money laundering scam. He donated the money to Israel. That is the reason he became a citizen of Paraguay. In 1974 he became aware of a clandestine organization operating in Argentina, Bolivia, Brazil, Chile, Equator, Paraguay, Peru and Uruguay using assassinations and coups to rid their countries of left wing influences."

"Sounds political and very down and dirty."

"It was! The whole thing was crystalized in November of 1974 when the US pledged to financially and materially support that operation. This was under the direction of President Nixon, and later, Ford. Nixon's doctrine to rid the Americas of Communism isn't a secret."

"What did your father do?"

"When he found out that the Nazis had a huge hand

in that stinking operation, he made it his personal battle. He held a big meeting in 1975 with all the members of our "Association." That's the name of our group. They all agreed to use whatever funds were necessary to throw a wrench into the works. Dad made trips to South America on a regular basis to continue the confidence game with the Nazis. All the while he used Nazi money to thwart the death squads from Argentina, Paraguay, Uruguay and Chile, and to a lesser extent, Bolivian squads. He spent a lot of money to overthrow Paraguayan President Alfredo Stroessner in 1989. He was really mad when he found out that the Secretary of State Henry Kissinger was one of the proponents of the operation given his German/Jewish heritage. The CIA gave lists of suspects and other intelligence while the FBI searched the US for individuals wanted by the Chilean Secret Police (DINA)."

"That's quite a lot to absorb."

"Wikipedia has a really good article on Operation Condor. Read it when you get a chance."

"I will, can you think of anything else that we haven't covered?"

"No, not right now, but I have your contact information. I won't be a stranger. Oh yes, just an aside, has the "Association" contracted someone to keep tabs on me."

"No, we have been keeping tabs on you by way of the people you have been interviewing. We inform everyone when you contact someone in our group."

"No trackers on my car or computer hacks?"

"Nope."

"Good to hear, I thank you for the information and Mrs. Tygart for the coffee."

"You're welcome," they both said and showed me to the door.

"Stay in Weggis for a couple of days, you might find it very enlightening."

"I will, it's a beautiful spot, good place to retire."

"Indeed."

I did exactly as he said and two days later an overnight letter arrived for me at my hotel. I opened it and smiled. The fact that they weren't following me gave me pause, who the hell cares what I was doing? Someone with deep pockets, the surveillance teams were first rate and wouldn't come cheap. One last thing and my mission would be complete.

CHAPTER 13

I SPENT A COUPLE MORE days in Weggis, on Ray's dime, of course. I took the train up to the top of Mt. Rigi and also to the top of Mt. Pilatus with a cable car ride down. Both were exhilarating trips, the views were stupendous. I arrived back in the States on June 3rd and landed at Palm Beach International Airport that evening. I spent the next day getting myself and my information together. My nephew, Rod, and I talked this morning and arranged to meet at his house in Manalapan this afternoon.

I arrived at the gate where the Manalapan security guard phoned Rod to make sure I was expected. Manalapan takes up half of Hypoluxo Island in the Lake Worth Lagoon and the entire beach front from Ocean Avenue in Lantana to the Boynton Inlet. I drove to Rod's house on Lands End Road, which I guessed, by its age, was his stepfather's house before he passed away. The house was modest, in a neighborhood that sported 20,000 square foot mansions, which made Rod's house pretty nice, if you know what I mean. I knocked on the door and Rod opened it almost immediately.

"Hi Uncle Nick, come on in." I stepped inside and was surprised at how big the place was. It looked much smaller from the outside.

"Hi Rod, I've finally got some information for you that I hope you are going to like."

"Great! We can go out by the pool and I'll pour some wine-give us something to do with our hands."

"Sounds good to me." I sat down at the small table on the patio facing the house next door, which was about the size of a Holiday Inn, and on my right was the Lagoon. Across the water was the shoreline and the houses that were 1000 miles out of my price range and they were in Hypoluxo, not Manalapan. Rod's dad did pretty well for himself.

Rod, dressed in shorts and a sleeveless tee shirt, set down two glasses of red wine on the table and sat down. "Enlighten me, please."

"Have you read the account of the robbery by Big Joe, Oddball, Kelly and Crapgame that I sent you?"

"Sure have, quite a story to say the least. Did you figure out who was who in the movie?"

I handed him several sheets of paper that I had printed up, revealing the real names of each of the individuals depicted in the movie. "With this list you can match each one of the characters in the movie to the real people in the "Association."Crapgame and Oddball came up with the names in the manuscript to cover up the identities of everyone involved in the heist. They just wanted to get the story out without putting the people involved in harm's way from the authorities, or the Nazis: both seem to have long memories."

I explained what Crapgame's son had told me and about my tour of Weggis. He hung on every word. I knew he was waiting for the part that dealt with his father.

"So, was Dad involved, which one of the guys in the movie was he?"

"They didn't show him in the movie, only a mention in passing, but he played a key role."

"Who was he in the movie?"

"Izzy."

"Izzy, who the hell is Izzy?"

"If you remember the movie, when Kelly gave Crapgame the gold bar and told him there were fourteen thousand of them?"

"Yes."

"Crapgame went batshit crazy and told Kelly he was beautiful and to help himself to the booze on the counter."

"Yes."

"Crapgame made a call on the field phone to Izzy and asked him for the price of gold on the Paris Exchange, which I'm sure he meant the Swiss National Bank (SNB) in Bern, Switzerland. The Paris Exchange didn't get going until much later."

"So, Izzy, was he some sort of clerk in headquarters?"

"He worked in the Personnel Section of the 35th Division and he was just as well connected as Crapgame. In fact they were partners in Crapgame's enterprises."

"Really?"

"Yup, what your dad did was bring Little Joe, Cowboy, Willard, Babra, Jonesey and Fischer back into the Recon Troop. He did the paperwork to leave Kelly, Big Joe, Gutowski, Penn, Petuko, Job, Mitchell and Grace as Missing in Action. Then he arranged for them to get Bronze Stars for the action with the Mark VI between Coincourt and Parrot, France. He also declared Job, Mitchell and Grace "presumed dead." He made up temporary records for all five of them giving them names of men that were Killed in Action. Izzy also was able to put Oddball, Turk, Wally, Moriarty, Rocky and Jesse back into the 737th Tank Battalion and change them from MIA status to RTD (Returned to Duty). He got Bronze Star medals for the battle at the French village of Framboise for Whiskey, Wally, Jesse, Murph, Chuck, and Oddball's entire crew. He showed that was where Murph and Chuck had been killed, instead of Schirmeck. Izzy was a genius with the paperwork and was given a full share in the gold along with the families of the men who had actually been killed."

"Wow, so Dad did participate!"

"Yes, in a big way. The entire group would have been in real trouble if Izzy hadn't been there. He also submitted the initial paperwork to headquarters about Big Joe's Recon Troop taking off toward the German Lines and being caught in a hellacious artillery barrage that had been called in by someone using Patton's call sign. The report had appeared to be signed by Maitland, the Troop Commander."

"Slick to say the least."

"The pen and the sword both seem to have equal weight in this instance." I filled him in on what had happened to each one of the men after the war. They had all gone into business, mostly fast food, laundromats, auto parts stores, car dealerships, trucking companies and gas stations. Some had been successful in the oil business. All their endeavors had been financed by the bank in Switzerland through a venture capital firm in the Bahamas. The company is called Golden Calf Ventures and it is owned by all the participants."

"What does that mean for me?"

"You have access to a no interest loan whenever you want it with the stipulation that you will pay it back when you can."

"Why didn't my stepfather tell me any of this?"

"I would say because you were living with your mother and you barely knew each other. Also, how did he know you would be interested?"

"You're right, I barely knew him, but always wanted to. My mother didn't want me to have anything to do with him.

Also, how do they ever make any money giving out *no interest, pay back, when you can loans*?"

"They don't, the interest was paid back in 1944 by brave men who took a chance and succeeded. The bank has many other income streams."

"Did Oddball and Crapgame make any money on the idea for the movie?"

"No, not directly, I think they did it to immortalize their comrades in arms without telling everything. It was sort of an interim thing until they could tell the whole story."

"When will that be?"

"They didn't tell me, but you'll know when you get a copy of the book."

CHAPTER 14

MONDAY, SEPTEMBER 17, 2018
IRS Headquarters Building
1111 Constitution Ave. NW
Washington, DC

DAVID WEEKLEY WALKED INTO THE conference room on the second floor and quickly noted that Special Agent in Charge Phillip Moseley hadn't arrived yet. His team, John Garrett and Terri Lyons, were seated with paper coffee cups in front of them. They all showed the wear and tear of the last four months and knew that their boss, Moseley, wasn't going to be pleased with the outcome of their investigation.

John and Terri greeted David with a "Good Morning",

but couldn't muster much else. They had all been up until two this morning putting the finishing touches on the 200 page report. It would be up to David to brief Moseley on what the boss referred to as the "meat of the situation."

Moseley breezed into the conference room in his customary confident/arrogant manner in his J Crew suit; Moseley strutted like he was wearing Armani. Being a federal employee didn't allow for a better suit along with his other expenses: rent, food or transportation. Moseley didn't realize that the investigators in the room were aware of that.

"Well, how are you all on this beautiful day?"

"Okay," came the reply almost in unison. It was expected, even if it wasn't true. After an 18 hour day and three hours of sleep it was anything but okay.

"How is the investigation coming along?"

"We think it is best to close it out at this point." Dave's voice was not as convincing as it should have been. He was speaking for the entire team and he had just gained the Assistant Agent in Charge designation last week. He headed the International Investigations Team and Terri was the assistant to the team leader responsible for investigating violations of the Bank Secrecy Act. John was head of an auditing team from the IRS facility at Martinsburg, West Virginia: a lot of talent and experience in a small package.

"What is that supposed to mean?" Moseley was somewhat peeved as the team had expected.

"We've got nothing, zip, nada sir. We have been at this investigation over ten months *and* the bill is now running close to a million dollars *and* we haven't found any wrongdoing so far *and* it's time to call it quits."

"Give me the rundown." Moseley cringed inside at the mention of the million dollar price tag with no results. This fact alone put the onus on him and he knew that the three people in the room with him had just put the ball in his court. Any further expenditure without tangible results would reflect on his record.

"Run it down for me."

"You know that the lawyer in New Orleans, Hugh Roberts, notified us he had reason to believe that there was a great deal of money being sent to the States via Switzerland and this guy Nick Wallach was involved in the operation. Roberts told the interviewer in New Orleans that he felt like the numbers were in the tens of millions. It got our attention."

"Did you initiate surveillance?"

"Naturally, I also brought Terri on board to start looking into any Swiss banking connection. The guy was pretty smart; he spotted our surveillance on day three and he played us until he wanted to disappear. He was able to go dark six times for a span of 24 to 36 hours, but we were able to track down who he had talked to or had met. The one time he lost us completely was when he went to San Diego: he disappeared for 78 hours. We also discovered he had hacked our internet connection in Ft. Pierce, Florida. That was a wakeup call and we need to guard against that in the future."

"Were you able to get anything on him or investigate who he talked to?"

"Yes sir, we were able to get each one of his contacts and do a thorough background to include a complete audit on each one and their business interests."

"How?"

"His rental cars, we got each car after he turned them in and downloaded their GPS histories and there it was, a good road map of his travels. He's good, but we are better. I'm sure we may have missed someone, but we still have enough to extrapolate the other players from the background investigations of the people we knew about."

"What about all the business and personal tax returns for all his contacts?"

"What about them," questioned John?

"If we can get something on one of them for personal or business fraud, we can pressure him or her to give up someone else and so on."

Smiling like the cat that ate the canary, John countered, "Very good strategy, but not possible in this case."

"Why?"

"In my entire career I have never seen a group of tax returns that were so precise and so correct they could defy the efforts of the most experienced auditor to find anything wrong. I have had 20 auditors going over the returns of all the people back to the early 50's and found only one that is suspect. And, that one is really very thin."

"Why not start with that one and move up the ladder?"

Again, Richard smiled that knowing smile before he lowered the boom on Moseley's attempt to salvage the investigation,

"It is RTM, as he is known to the group. He is clean as a whistle until six months after his wife's death, or murder, I should say. He and his son disappeared after several Cartel types met untimely ends. According to the FBI report, they are both suspects in the torture and murder of several low level Cartel soldiers. Sadly, they both crossed the border at Tijuana on June the 21st of last year and have yet to surface."

"How are they living, are they drawing money from their assets in the States?"

"No sir, not a penny. I contacted a friend of mine at Langley last week and he said, off the record, that the pair has popped up on their radar and they want to talk to them, too. It seems that they are still on a spree and have collared and dispatched several individuals that are key players in Langley's drug operations in Costa Rica and Panama."

"Have you contacted the FBI with a formal request?"

"Yes sir, back in April when the investigation first started to get serious. They ran down the background of every one of these guys and found that six of them came back home after the war using names and records of guys that were Killed in Action."

"That's it! We get them on Identity Theft charges and squeeze 'em to rat on the others."

"Brilliant Idea, sir, and we could go after them with the full weight of the Justice Department, except the first law making Identity Theft a crime was passed in 1998. The Sixth Amendment makes it illegal to prosecute a person for a crime that was committed before the act became illegal."

"What about Golden Calf Ventures in the Bahamas and the bank in Switzerland, anything there?"

"Nothing there-everything is above board, just like the rest of the operation." David handed Moseley the FBI report as he answered.

"Shit! So what you're telling me, in essence, is the only people who we could possibly get anything on are torturing and killing people in Central and possibly South America. I feel sure that if they are caught, squeezing them for an IRS fraud case will pale next to murder charges. And, that is, if Langley brings them in and doesn't just kill them and be done with it."

All three smiled and nodded their heads.

"Close it down, we'll have to eat the million. Maybe as a consolation prize, look into this lawyer in New Orleans, maybe he's dirty."

Again, they all three smiled and David said, "already in the works."

EPILOGUE

Present Day
West Palm Beach, FL

I WAS GIVEN PERMISSION TO publish this book on the 80th Anniversary of the German Unconditional surrender of May 7, 1945. All the participants in the "heist" have passed away. The statute of limitations has run out on any crimes associated with the robbery, except the failure to report income by Big Joe and his son. Their story may be told at a later date.

The families of the individuals involved can't be held responsible for what their fathers did and the money that they made from the legitimate loans by a venture capital firm can't be questioned because they were all legal. All taxes have been paid. In the case of Big Joe and his son, the Association made sure that all legalities were followed and taxes paid. However, what Big Joe and his son are suspected of doing, in relation to killings in New York, Central America, and South America is just that, suspicions and nothing more. Big Joe disappeared from Manhattan on December 31, 1995 and was declared dead January 15, 2003. He was born on November 9, 1917, so today, if he were still alive, he would be 107 years old. It is highly unlikely that he is still alive, and if he is, he wouldn't survive extradition or a trial. His son is a different story, there is no further information about his condition or whereabouts.

This is a novel, parts of it are true and parts of it came out of the author's mind. To loosely paraphrase the CIA's oft used words, I can neither confirm nor deny which parts of the story are true and which are fabrications. You have to find out for yourselves.

I read a novel a long time ago, *Mila 18,* by Leon Uris. He said that parts of the book were true and parts were fiction. The book was published in 1961 and I read it in 1969. I questioned, along with other readers, *what was true and what was false?* When I lived in Germany (1971-1974) I used to go to the City Library in Fulda and there were several books in English in a special section. I found out later that they were donated by people in the Army that were stationed at Downs Barracks in Fulda. One of the books, and I will tell you up front that I don't remember the title or the author, but it was written in 1952 by a Jewish survivor of the Warsaw Ghetto. Reading that gentleman's book was like reading *Mila 18*. It was apparent that Uris' entire book had been lifted from this man's work and the *original* work was apparently based on facts. The account was surely written from his remembrances and people who lived during that period. So, I have concluded that just about everything in *Mila 18* was true: Uris even included several of the thoughts and conversations from the 1952 work.

As with all things in this world, don't take my word for it, *Search for Yourself!*

ABOUT THE AUTHOR

ROBERT "BOB" WHEELER is a retired military/civilian helicopter and airplane pilot. He is a Certified Helicopter Instructor and an Instrument Flight Examiner. During Bob's 39-year military career he had combat tours in Vietnam, Desert Storm, and Afghanistan. He has done extensive research helping to locate missing helicopter crews in Vietnam. This is his second novel; the first was *Amelia Earhart Betrayed*. Both novels are available on Amazon.com.

www.ingramcontent.com/pod-product-compliance
Lightning Source LLC
Chambersburg PA
CBHW050505260626
47157CB00004B/1202